PRAISE
THE WINNING S

This ['Gabriel's Halo'] is a story brimming with good things all the way through. I love the ending, which reverberates with hope. We don't have too much to worry about as long as Oswald and Gabriel are still on the job.
- *Lorraine Mace, Head Judge, Writers' Forum, November 2016*

Rhiannon Lewis's 'The Jugs Stay with the Dresser' was the stand-out entry for me in this year's Frome Festival Short Story Competition. A vivid, poignant story of a young wife in 60s' rural Wales who finds her voice and discovers an unlikely ally along the way. Beautifully written with plenty of sweet to balance the bitter, it will stay with me for a long time.
- *Laura Wilkinson, Author and Frome Festival's Short Story Competition Judge, 2017*

Lewis's story was the next-to-last story that I read, and I knew immediately that it ['Piano Solo'] was the winner. Lewis brilliantly describes Walter's emotional performance in such vivid detail that the reader experiences the risks and the exhilaration that accompanies, not only a job well done, but a genius performance.
- *Anita Bryan, Judge for the short story category of the William Faulkner Literary Contest, 2020*

Also by Rhiannon Lewis

My Beautiful Imperial

Rhiannon Lewis

I Am the Mask Maker
and other stories

Rhiannon Lewis

I Am the Mask Maker
and other stories

Victorina Press
www.victorinapress.com

Typesetting and layout: Jorge Vasquez
Cover design: Tríona Walsh
Cover artwork: ©1996 *Javi* by David Hopkins
Reproduction: Dean Brannagan Photography

British Library Cataloguing in Publication Data
A catalogue record for this book is available from the
British Library.

ISBN: 978-1-9169057-0-2

Typeset in 11pt Garamond
Printed and bound in Great Britain by 4edge Ltd

I Ffion Leonie

A NOTE ON THE TEXT

The stories in this collection are arranged, generally, in chronological order. Some of them have been successful in literary competitions and have been published previously in those competition anthologies.

'Gabriel's Halo' won first prize in the monthly short story competition held by Writers' Forum, and was published in the November 2016 edition of the magazine.

'The Jugs Stay with the Dresser' won first prize in Frome Festival's short story competition, 2017.

'Piano Solo' won first prize in the short story category of the William Faulkner Literary Contest, 2020, held in New Albany, Mississippi; the first UK story to win the contest since the competition was established in 1997.

'At a Junction' came third in the Hammond House International Literary Prize, 2017, and was published by Hammond House in *Eternal: Award Winning Short Stories*.

'The Significance of Swans' was shortlisted by the Bristol Prize, 2018, and published by Tangent Books in the *Bristol Short Story Prize Anthology, Volume 11*.

'The Last Flight of La Librairie d'Afrique du Nord' was shortlisted by the H.G. Wells Short Story Competition, 2020, and published by St Ursin Press, in *Vision*.

CONTENTS

GABRIEL'S HALO

The queue at the temporary desk for decommissioned halos had eventually shrunk down to one. It was the end of the day and all the angels whose names started with 'G' had been and gone. One by one, they had shuffled past a series of signs: *Returning halos ONLY, Please form an orderly queue! STRICTLY all general enquiries to the information desk*. There was one more angel in front and then Gabriel would be the last. He turned to see whether anyone else had arrived but there was no one. Above him, the sky was still blue although darkening a little. The clouds were a thousand shades of white. They hovered and floated.

Eventually, a voice from the desk said, 'Well there, Gabriel,' and he turned to see Angel Oswald, arms wide, leaning forward on the counter. Oswald was wearing his usual pale grey work overalls but on the right-hand pocket flap there was an unfamiliar badge which said, *Head of Halo Reclamation – temporary*.

'Hey, Oswald,' replied Gabriel and, despite his best effort, let out a long sigh. He stepped up to the desk and placed his halo on the thick pile of shining tissue paper that lay on the glass counter.

'Ah,' said Oswald, smiling. Already, the halo's brilliant glow had diminished; the golden hue was being overtaken by a bluish tinge, its smoothness was turning grainy, almost, the iridescence becoming matt.

'Aa-ah,' said Oswald again. His voice was deep and fatherly.

'What do they look like? Eventually?' asked Gabriel.

'Well,' said Oswald, turning his head slightly but keeping his eyes fixed on the object in front of him, 'I don't rightly know. They've been around a lot longer than I have, and whenever we've had a defective one, or one in need of maintenance, well, the light has never really gone out of it altogether. The worst one I ever saw was the colour of a perfectly ripe Victoria plum – you know, when they're very fresh, and they have a kind of dust on them that you wipe off on your sleeve to make them shiny.'

'Oh,' said Gabriel.

Oswald's hair was looking particularly unruly that day. His crown was hair-free and surprisingly tanned, but the rest of his head was covered in long, wiry, dazzling-white hair, which grew outwards horizontally, lending him the air of someone in a perpetual state of shock. He reminded Gabriel of a brilliant, curmudgeonly archaeologist he had once known – slightly ruffled, always on the verge of a great discovery.

'This was always one of the better looking ones, of course,' said Oswald, extending his arm under the counter and bringing out a white cardboard box. 'People assumed they were all pretty much the same, but they weren't, you know – not at all. Some glowed peach, others had a bit of lavender in them. This one had a kind of resonance, like it had a piece of music moving through it.' Oswald licked the tips of his fingers and was about to draw up the corners of the tissue when he hesitated.

'Why don't you put it on, Gabriel? One last time, for me to see?'

'Well… '

'It won't take a moment and there's no one waiting now.'

'I suppose… '

Oswald let go of the tissue, and placed his hands around the halo. 'Oh, it's all coming back to me now. It's heavier than you think, isn't it? And it has the texture of a warm block of ice,' he said, with delight. 'Stand back!'

Gabriel did as he was told, and gathered his long sleeves about him. Oswald held the halo in his right hand, balanced it, then drawing his right arm across himself, and with the lightest flick of the wrist, sent it flying up above Gabriel's head. He'd put a bit of spin on it, Gabriel noticed, but once it found its place, it settled, rotating gracefully. It came to life – brilliant rays of light bounced off the clouds around them.

Oswald slid his hands into his overall pockets and grinned with satisfaction. 'Take a look in the mirror!'

Oh, no, I'd rather not, thought Gabriel. He had gone through the same rigmarole that morning – putting on his best gown, setting his halo straight, gazing at his sad reflection in the dormitory mirror, taking it off for the final time (or so he thought), with a heavy heart.

Oswald produced a mirror. 'There!' He crossed his arms, and left it suspended in mid-air. He always seemed to have an uncanny knack of placing halos just so. Whenever Gabriel did it, it never quite looked the same. Perhaps Oswald set them at a slightly jaunty angle? With his face illuminated like this, all the nooks and crannies were evened out, the dark shadows under his eyes and the deep hollows of his cheeks were erased. He seemed young again.

'Not so scary, really,' laughed Oswald.

That old joke, thought Gabriel. He was well aware of his terrifying reputation. He hadn't meant to be terrifying. The issue was partly to do with timing. He was always compelled to appear at moments that were, for many people, not entirely auspicious. And, bafflingly, people expected him to have a kind of benign, wishy-washy blondness. They were invariably surprised to discover that he was dark-eyed and rather glowering. One of the novice angels once told him that his 'resting face' was unusually severe. Not much I can do about it, he'd thought, although he had tried to smile a little more often after that.

So there he was, smiling at his smiling self. It was all an illusion of course. He reached up, removed the halo, and handed it back to Oswald. The light reflected on the clouds was extinguished, and everything was darker than before.

'Where will they all go?'

'They'll be sent back to central storage for safe keeping – in case they're ever needed.' Oswald licked his fingertips and drew up the layers of tissue. 'It's all climate control and whatnot over there now. They shouldn't come to any harm. I dare say they'll come out looking as good as new.'

If they're ever needed, thought Gabriel. He watched as Oswald turned the halo over deftly, enveloping it with rustling paper. It glowed wistfully, and Gabriel felt a painful dart of anguish shoot through him.

'What about you, Oswald? Where will you go?'

Oswald began scrunching sheets of tissue into large balls. 'Oh, nowhere just yet. We have a few more weeks to go. Tomorrow, we're on the "H"s and "I"s. You wouldn't believe the names we've had! Gabriel's a nice name for an angel, I think. But Grosmont?' Oswald chuckled. 'Greeber!' He laughed, and packed the tissue balls into the corners of the box. 'Greengage!' They could be here for quite a while, thought Gabriel.

'And that's just the boys! Then there's the cataloguing, and the storage. Yes, we'll be here for a few weeks yet. But afterwards,' he said, folding his arms, 'well, believe it or not, I fancy going to New England. They say the folks are decent. I know a lake with a cabin, which would do me just fine. I'll hide myself away – become a fisher of fish.' Oswald patted the halo absently and gazed past Gabriel with the faraway look of someone who was thinking about his first catch of the day. 'Course, I've never been a travelling angel like you, so I can't be sure. It's all a bit of an adventure.' He picked up the halo and placed it in its paper cocoon.

Adventure, thought Gabriel. Is that what it was? Their being decommissioned was the one thing he could never have foreseen. They had all laughed at the first rumours but soon stopped when they realised the officials were serious. The angels had become an irrelevance, it seemed. No one believed in them anymore. Apparently, the last person to sense their existence had died in a bizarre accident involving an umbrella stand and a Swiss pianist. To Gabriel's thinking, it had all been more than a little suspicious.

'Do you believe them, Oswald?'

Oswald was making more tissue balls, and for a moment Gabriel thought he was deliberately ignoring his question. Eventually, Oswald shook his head, and let out a slow whistle through his teeth. 'There's no reason to doubt them,' he whispered.

'*Them.* That's another thing! Who are *they*, Oswald? Who's in charge, now? I mean, we haven't had any direct dealings with *Him* for a very long time, not since… well, to be honest, I can't remember when.'

More and more layers of tissue were being scrunched. Oswald whispered reluctantly, 'They say there's a new pet project.'

The halo seemed to give one last desperate glimmer through the shining layers. Then Oswald closed the lid. Gabriel was gripped by an awful dread. He had an overwhelming urge to grab the box and run away with it. He steadied himself against the counter and hoped the urge would go away. Oswald reached down and brought out a heavy dispenser, complete with luminous yellow tape. It landed on the counter with a thud.

'He *knew* I was there, Oswald.'

Oswald groaned. Gabriel had told him this story, many times already, of how, only days before the final declaration of decommissioning, he had saved a farmer and his baby girl from certain death at a junction.

'He told everyone, Oswald – his wife, his children, his neighbours!'

'No one believed him!'

'That's not the point. He *knew* I was there.'

'He was being fanciful.'

5

'I don't think so.'

'You don't *think* so?'

'I know so, Oswald. And if he knew I was there, it means the decommissioning can't be right. It's based on a false premise!'

Oswald hunched his shoulders as if expecting a huge thunderbolt to come hurtling in his direction at any moment. 'You're just upset,' he hissed, furiously pulling and tearing strips of tape, and sticking them down on the lid. 'It's understandable. It's to be expected. It's natural, after all this time.'

The angels paused and looked down at the box. It was almost unrecognisable, covered in thick tramways of lurid tape.

Oswald sighed. 'I've had enough, Gabriel. I just want to go fishing.'

Gabriel placed his hand on the box. The light had gone but still he could feel its warmth, like a beating heart. His friend was right. They had to accept the inevitable. He patted the box tenderly and hoped that the halo could sense his parting touch through the layers of tissue and cardboard and thick, sticky-tape.

'We worked our socks off, Oswald.'

'I know.'

'What more could we have done?'

'Nothing, Gabriel. You all did your best.'

A shiny trolley had appeared. Oswald lifted the box with the halo in it and placed it on top.

Gabriel imagined himself leaping athletically over the counter and absconding with the swaddled box. 'I bet the other side's not being decommissioned?'

'Seems they've also gone off to the new project,' whispered Oswald. 'They like a challenge.'

It wasn't too late, thought Gabriel, glancing at the trolley. Surely, Oswald wouldn't stop him? But Oswald reached forward and gripped his hand so firmly that it brought Gabriel to his senses.

'Look me up in New England. You'll find me. I'll be the one with the largest basket of fish.'

They shook hands. 'Oswald – you take care now.'

Gabriel turned away from the desk to make his way back to the dormitories. The evening light was fading fast. He paused for a moment to watch the sun's last rays on the billowing clouds. Then, just as he was about to move off, he noticed something strange. Something brushed against his cheek. He brought his hands to his face. He was amazed. It was a breeze. There had never been a breeze in Heaven. The clouds moved, not like earthly weather clouds but of their own accord. They were not dictated to by climactic conditions. Something was changing. And, as if one strange thing was not enough, he realised there was a second thing. There was a sound – a low moan, like the sound of a rising wind through a great tree that has lost its leaves. The sound of absence. The sound of a door blown open, with no one left to close it.

Gabriel turned to tell Oswald, but Oswald had already gone. A makeshift sign stood on the counter. It said, *Open again at 9am SHARP for 'H's and 'I's only.* Gabriel pulled his gown around him, shivered, and walked on.

So, it was all over. Oh, he knew what the angels were saying, that it was just a short-term state of affairs. They would soon get a call, or a sign. But the ache in the pit of his belly didn't feel transitory. It felt like a wrongness that had settled in for the long haul.

Distracted, Gabriel's boot caught in the hem of his gown and he nearly tripped over his own feet. His hand shot up to stop the halo from toppling, but his fingers swished through empty air. He paused. The setting sun seemed to be melting, pouring precious metals into the sky, and gilding the edges of the world. He watched the colours ripple and flow all around. For a moment, he thought he could actually feel his heart breaking. You need to get a grip, he thought, tying his belt a little tighter.

That's when he heard the noise, like wings flapping. He hitched up his gown and walked on. Everyone knew it was a myth – this idea that angels had wings. It had been concocted long ago, to explain how they could move around so quickly. Gabriel thought it was funny how at any other point in history, their skills would have been attributed to the use of roller skates, or jet skis or hovercraft.

There it was again, that irritating sound. He stopped and turned just in time to see Oswald running, red-faced, towards him.

'Come on!' Oswald hissed, as he hurtled past, his baggy overalls flapping. Gabriel had never seen Oswald running. He wasn't really designed for it. It was a kind of lolloping action, made more lopsided by his awkward cargo. Gabriel stared after him, his mouth gaping as he realised what Oswald was carrying under his arm. There was no mistaking the neon-coloured sticky tape on the cardboard box.

'Don't just... *stand* there!' gasped Oswald, disappearing between the clouds.

Gabriel gathered up his gown and sprinted after him.

'What's going on?'

'Fish!'

He's losing his marbles, thought Gabriel. He would have to keep up with him just to make sure that he didn't come to any harm.

'All that talk... about fishing... got me thinking,' Oswald wheezed. 'You're right. There's something... decidedly... fishy... going on.'

Gabriel watched the box as it bobbed up and down under Oswald's lurching arm. On Oswald's back, there was a brand new rucksack. It pitched from side to side, slightly out of time with the box, and the whole ensemble gave Oswald the look and sound of a fleeing one-man-band, escaping from an aggravated audience. And, unless Gabriel was mistaken, he could just make out the distinctive, radiating circle of Oswald's own halo tucked safely inside.

'Got to… make a run for it!' Oswald puffed, as he jettisoned the box with a fling. Gabriel reached out and caught it with his outstretched fingertips.

'I thought we were supposed to… hand them in? I thought we were being… put out to pasture? Pensioned off? Retired? Dis – charged?'

'You have to… make a stand!'

'What?'

'Don't worry. I'll help you… with the practicalities… the resources… that kind of thing. You'll have to come up with the strategy. You're the brains. Tactics, lines of attack… I'm no good at that stuff. I know how you feel, Gabriel… but you're not quite finished. You've been out of the river too long. I reckon… you need to get off the bank… and back into the white water.'

Oswald stopped abruptly, and Gabriel skidded to a halt, just missing him, causing a flurry of small clouds to whirl around them.

'This is the spot,' wheezed Oswald.

Gabriel fell backwards, hugging the cardboard box to his chest. It had taken months to get used to the decommissioning, and here was Oswald turning everything upside down again. Surely, this was even worse – nebulous, uncertain hope, instead of cast-iron despair? Gabriel was about to utter a string of banned expletives when he felt the box being wrenched from his hands. Oswald, already wearing his own halo, was wielding a glinting fisherman's penknife in the direction of the gaudy sticky tape. Within seconds, the box was opened, and Gabriel's halo was released into the air. It settled, triumphantly, over his head.

Oswald peered through the layers of cloud beneath

their feet. 'Look at it, Gabriel. How beautiful it is!' Sunlight caught the edges of the parting mists, and far beneath them they could see a dizzying patchwork of fields in every shade of enamelled green and gold. Here and there, small towns and villages were scattered. Rivers twisted and glinted like polished wire. Sprawling cities sparkled. 'They need us now, more than ever. We can't just abandon them.'

'They abandoned us!' wailed Gabriel, dizzy with a cocktail of incompatible emotions – fear, excitement, love, disdain. His heart thundered in his chest.

'This is no time to be pedantic,' said Oswald laying an ominous hand on Gabriel's sleeve.

'We have no authority!' whispered Gabriel, drawing his face close to Oswald's. 'We'd be going against the flow!'

Oswald's eyes glistened with excitement as he grasped Gabriel's shoulder. 'Like two salmon!'

Gabriel heard something about holding on to his halo, and before he knew it, they were plummeting towards the earth, tumbling arm in arm, through layer upon layer, upon layer of heavenly cloud.

THE JUGS STAY WITH THE DRESSER

Marion looked down at her hands in the washing-up bowl. They were covered in suds – again. She paused and then looked up at the marbled tiles on the wall in front of her and thought, it was a man, obviously – the person who designed this house. This kitchen. Particularly the location of this sink. What woman with half a brain – who has to have her hands in suds ten times a day – would put a sink against a solid wall? Even if the walls were covered in tiles? The tiles were horrible too, if she was being totally honest, even though she'd help choose them. The best mid-price turquoise tiles they could afford in the local mercantile shop, just after they married five years earlier – in 1962. Even that purchase had to be negotiated, she remembered. That was the problem with moving in to your father-in-law's farm. You're not the mistress of your own house. You're a long way down the pecking-order of father-in-law, husband, cows. Even the opinion of the long-dead mother-in-law still held sway. 'Maggie wouldn't like the tiles... ' Marion stared at them and wondered if those were shapes of faces she could see? Frozen in the ceramic.

She sank her hands under the suds again and pulled out a heavy blue and white striped mug. It had definitely seen better days. The edge was chipped in places and the inside was permanently stained. On the underside – when she wiped off the bubbles – she could see the words 'Genuine Cornishware' stamped underneath. His special mug. When did he ever go to Cornwall, she wondered? She doubted whether the father-in-law had ever been further than Carmarthen. All of thirty miles away. And when she'd suggested one day that perhaps the mug should be thrown out on account of the germs that could be lurking in the unglazed chips, the mulish silence that greeted her was all the answer she needed. The tatty mismatching thing would be there until the day of reckoning. Unless it broke, of course. She turned it over in the suds and wondered how fragile it really was. He was seventy-six and never had a day's illness in all his life, so he liked to remind them from time to time. She would be washing this chipped thing for a while she reckoned – in front of this wall.

Partly out of devilment, she said suddenly,

'When we win the football pools what do you think about getting a kitchen extension and putting the sink by the window?' Marion paused and listened for telltale signs of dissent rustling between the folds of the Sunday newspapers at the kitchen table. She stared at the wall again and was sure she could see the shadow of her own likeness emerging from the marbling. It grimaced.

'Yes, that would be good,' said her husband meekly. He knew his place in the order too.

Then the father-in-law coughed the little cough he made when he couldn't bring himself to disagree. He disagreed all the same. His lungs were disconcerted. Then the kitchen settled back down into its rustling Sunday afternoon silence. The face in the tile feigned surprise as if to say, what on earth were you thinking – moving in with two stubborn men, set in their ways? You won't be the mistress here for years.

Just as Marion was putting the last of the mismatched cups on the draining rack, there came a commotion from the passageway. Two small children came running in – the eldest a girl and a boy not much younger.

'Baby's awake!' said the first.

'The cowboys and Indians have woken it,' said the other. Bloody John Wayne thought Marion and right on cue there was a wail. Soon it would be time to wash nappies – another round of buckets and Napisan. The face in the turquoise marbling was really laughing now.

The father-in-law's brother had died. A widower, he and his wife had been childless and the house was being cleared. Now that the father-in-law was the eldest of the remaining clan, he was to have first refusal of the contents.

The day of clearance had arrived. Marion was at the sink again, dealing with the breakfast dishes and listening to the conversation. There was a discussion about baler twine and cardboard boxes. Then out of the blue, says the father-in-law,

'You'll need to take the trailer and some ropes.'

Marion's hands paused in the soapy water.

'Why, Father? What is it you want to take?' she heard her husband ask.

'Well, for once, I'm going to have my own way.'

Marion raised her eyebrows at the faces in the tiles and thought, well that's rich, coming from him.

'I'd like to have the dresser.'

The dresser! Handed down through God knows how many generations, all the way down from the ark!

'Aunty will never let you have that,' said the husband. There was another long pause. The bubbles in the sink crackled and spat as they burst. They're having a laugh, Marion thought.

'She married in,' said the father-in-law. 'And their son has no children.'

Marion swilled the water over the dishes but not so loudly that she wouldn't be able to hear.

'I have grandchildren,' he added, 'and the eldest is a girl. The dresser has a future here.'

It was true, Marion nodded. Family tradition dictated – dresser to the eldest girl, farm to the eldest boy. Marion thought of her own circumstances. Her family's farm had been sold long ago and even if there had been a dresser, she'd been a long way down the pecking order there too.

'I never got my way anywhere when I was a lad,' he added, 'I'm seventy-six and I'm thinking it's high time.'

I'd like to see him try, thought Marion. Aunty had been a formidable piano teacher complete with matching sets of framed certificates. And then like a bolt from the blue, the old man said, 'Marion, I'd like you to come too, if you don't mind.'

With her hands still stuck in the plastic bowl she turned as far as she could and nodded. 'Right you are.' Honour your father and mother, father-in-law, cat, dog and milk bucket and all that, thought Marion. At least it would get her away from the wall.

'We'll make arrangements to take the dresser,' said Aunty as soon as they arrived. She was eighty-three and still straight as a die with her Harris-tweed pencil skirt wrapped around her bony hips, her leather-heeled brogues and her definitely un-simulated pearls. Marion was always impressed by the effort and thought well, that's the end of that. For all the father-in-law's bluster, the dresser was going elsewhere.

'No,' whispered the father-in-law and as softly spoken as he was, the comment reverberated around the parlour as if a neutron bomb had been detonated. 'With all due respect,' he added, gaining a bit of speed and volume as he went, 'your Jim doesn't have any children and my Tom has three. And my eldest grandchild is a girl.'

Marion straightened her cardigan. She had to hand it to him – he had guts. Aunty was as sharp-edged as ever. Even her pearls seemed lined up to attention. The father-in-law, all stooping seventy-six years of him, leaning on his wobbly walking stick, smelling of tobacco and Rizla papers, wasn't an obvious match for the woman's confrontational chin.

Everyone stared at the dresser or stared at their feet. Marion felt a surge of excitement. This was a change from the suds – a battle of wills, the likes of which had not been seen since the last dramatic episode of *Dixon of Dock Green* or *Peyton Place*.

'Well,' said Aunty, 'if that's how it is, we'll be having the jugs.' The father-in-law bowed his head and there was something in the gesture that made Marion think, yes, this is the way they've walked over him all along because he's polite. Banking on the fact that he wouldn't say boo to a goose. And for all his stubbornness she felt suddenly annoyed on his behalf. Any moment now, he might cave in and having come this far, Marion felt compelled to cut across and say, 'No,' a little louder than she meant to. 'The jugs stay with the dresser. That's the way it goes. There's no point in a dresser without any jugs. And the jugs are useless to you on their own.' Aunty glared at Marion, young mother of three, as if she was a rude eleven-year-old.

Stand your ground, stand your ground, thought Marion fingering the ribbed edge of her hand-knit cardigan. Another silence clattered around the parlour. On the mantelpiece, the four circulating brass balls of the carriage clock paused momentarily then turned tail and hurried the other way. In the glass case on top of the chest of drawers, the stuffed squirrel dared to bare its teeth at the owl. Then the father-in-law made his mulish little cough, which, for once, was a good sign. Good for you, old man, Marion thought. Aunty hadn't banked on the supporting troops. And it dawned on her then that he knew exactly what he was doing when he'd asked her to go with them. Well, I never, she thought. He guessed I'd stand up for him before I knew it myself!

'Better get packing then,' said Aunty, grabbing a pile of musty *Cambrian News* and dumping them in the middle of the floor. It seemed childish to jump up and down with glee after she left the room so the three of them packed in silence, jumping up and down in spirit. It was the most fun Marion had seen in months.

'Well,' he said. He was a man of few words.

The three of them stood in the sitting room staring at

the dust-free newcomer complete with freshly washed jugs all arranged in size order along the front. Marion thought of Aunty watching the trailer leaving – face puckered as if she'd been forced to eat a bag of sloes. It was a shock for some people to come second.

After the milking and another supper, Marion was back at the sink. The children had been put to bed and the last of the coal from the galvanized scuttle had been tipped into the top of the Rayburn for the night. Marion heard the father-in-law get up on his creaking knees.

'You should think about a kitchen extension,' she heard him say to her husband as he passed behind her on the way to bed.

'Yes,' came the surprised response. It was ridiculous of course. They all knew that there weren't two spare shillings to rub together. And even if there were, they'd be allocated to the shiny blue Leyland tractor that her husband had his eye on. But, still.

Marion looked down at the suds. They sparkled as the last dish emerged. It was the stripy blue Cornishware mug. She gave it an extra rinse under the tap and placed it carefully on the draining rack. She smiled at the marbled tiles then tipped the washing bowl over until the water swilled around the stainless steel sink, gurgled particularly loudly, and disappeared.

PIANO SOLO

Walter Wagstaff closed the brass clasp on his leather briefcase. It made a satisfying 'clunk'. He extended his right arm in front of him, then hinged at the elbow so that his jacket sleeve slid up his wrist just enough for him to see the watch face clearly. He estimated five minutes past five. He checked the dial. It was, in fact, three minutes past five. *Good.* The Year Thirteen simultaneous equation assignments had been better than expected, so he was two minutes in credit. This meant that even if the Headmaster caught him on the way out, wanting to discuss whatever was the current bugbear, he was unlikely to be home any later than twenty past five.

Walter picked up the briefcase, walked to the classroom door and switched off the lights. The internal corridor, which ran the length of B block, was bathed in the sickly light of fluorescent bulbs. A contract cleaner was occupied by a lonely waltz with the floor polisher, coaxing the machine from side to side in wide arcs. Walter was about to disappear through the doors at the top of the stairway when the man raised his head,

'You can't go down that way. They've put wax on the floor.'

Walter let go of the door handle and sighed. All this cleaning, yet the corridors always looked dusty. Perhaps the dust never went anywhere. Perhaps these people spent their evenings moving it from one place to the next just to give the illusion of cleaning. Walter retraced his steps. As he passed the man and his own classroom door, he checked his watch again. He had wasted nearly a minute and hadn't gone anywhere.

Walter descended two flights of stairs then paused. He could take the shorter route past the school offices, thereby risking an encounter with the Head. Or he could take the longer way around the quadrangle. Given that the Head seemed to enjoy prowling the school, notebook in hand, at the end of the day, and was just as likely to come across him in the corridor as anywhere else, Walter took the calculated risk of the shorter route. At least he was wearing his silent soft-soled shoes. Last term's noisy leather ones had been a mistake. He was forever being collared. 'Oh, Mr Wagstaff, the Head of Year wants this... ' 'Oh, Mr Wagstaff, the Year Ten grades... ' 'What are we going to do about Dean Bayliss?' Not to mention unwelcome comments from the worst elements of 12W, 'Waggie's wearing heels! Clippedy clop! Something you want to tell us, Mr Wag?'

Walter raised his chin defiantly and breathed a sigh of relief as he escaped unhindered into the car park. He passed through the school gates and made his way along Launceston Avenue. It was already dark. One of the street lights flickered, turned a shade of blue, then went out completely. As he approached, it came back on. On the opposite side of the avenue there were two boys making their way home. One was pushing what appeared to be a brand new bike. They dithered for a moment, and Walter saw the flash of a lighter flame followed by puffs of smoke. One of them was, in fact, the obnoxious Dean Bayliss. Walter pinned his gaze on the junction far ahead of him.

'Mr Wag!' Walter didn't break his stride.

'Hey, Waggy! You won't tell on us, will you? Sir?' They cackled. Even with his back turned, Walter could feel them brandishing their cigarettes. Years ago, he might have crossed the road to reason with them about the probable consequences. Those days were long gone. With his left hand, he buttoned up his coat – his Teflon exoskeleton.

Walter walked on, towards the busy junction with Northern Avenue. The road was one of the main routes in and out of the city. Headlights streamed past and the noise of traffic increased as he approached. A little further on, Walter's house on Ainge Terrace stood on the intersection between five roads. Built in the 1960s, the terrace looked like an experimental exercise. The oddly shaped houses were incongruous, squeezed on to a tight corner plot between rows of Victorian houses.

Walter arrived at the garden gate and checked his watch. Twenty-four minutes past five. He reached in to his coat pocket and took out his bunch of keys. The fob was a tarnished disk with the words 'Mafia Staff Car' engraved on it. A college friend had given it to him. It had not exactly been a present. Walter had exclaimed one day that he thought the slogan on it was amusing.

'Well, in that case, dear Wagstaff, you shall have it,' said the friend, releasing his own keys. 'Let's face it, mate, your world isn't exactly a bundle of laughs, is it?' At the time, Walter had accepted the key ring with enthusiasm. It was only afterwards that his feelings had become slightly mixed. Until then, it had never occurred to him that his world was any different from anyone else's. True, he had lost his father when he was still a toddler. Although, perhaps, 'lost' was not the right word. His father had disappeared. The circumstances had not been discussed. Walter had never seen a death certificate. His mother never spoke of him. The words 'run off' skittered across Walter's consciousness, but he turned his head away from the unpleasant image. He reached up to the lock and turned the key.

Walter stepped inside and closed the door. He placed his briefcase by the umbrella stand. The stand was made of brass and shaped like an upended half-opened umbrella. Walter looked at it. The strange contraption had been there ever since he could remember. No one ever put umbrellas in it. He wondered why they kept it. He leant over and peered into it. At the bottom there were three paperclips and two dead flies. He made a mental note that tomorrow, in between marking Year Ten projects and preparing reports, he would tip the dusty contents out of the front door.

Walter took off his coat and hung it on the hook. He took off his jacket but rather than hang this by the door he walked down the narrow hallway and entered the dining room. Beyond this was the small kitchen at the back of the house. His mother was standing with her back to him stirring something on the hob. It was Tuesday, so she would be putting the finishing touches to the casserole, thought Walter.

'Alright?' asked his mother, without turning to look.

'Yes, thank you,' said Walter, placing his jacket on the back of his dining chair so that the corners of the chair-back fitted perfectly into the shoulders. He looked up. Above the cooker was a battery-operated clock. It had a bottle-green plastic rim, and the face was covered with pictures of strange foreign vegetables like aubergines, peppers and chillies. Walter had brought it back from a school exchange to France. A gift from the host parents in anticipation of a reciprocal visit. In any case, the French child, Guillaume, had decided to stay with another pupil so the clock never really served its proper purpose. The hands, which were shaped like the tips of asparagus, showed twenty-six minutes to six.

Walter sat. He took the linen napkin from his plate and unfolded it on to his lap. He could hear his mother draining vegetables in the sink. She came out of the kitchen holding a casserole dish. Gurda Wagstaff was seventy-nine and still thin. She had never put on any middle-aged weight. Apart from the wrinkles and grey hair she looked pretty much as she had when Walter was a child. Then again, he thought, she'd been thirty-eight when she'd had him. No spring chicken.

She placed the casserole in the centre of the table on a mat which had a photograph of Lymington's funicular railway on it. Then she returned to the kitchen to fetch the vegetables. She placed a dish of new potatoes and sliced carrots on the table. Walter watched as a neat knob of butter slid slowly off the top-most potato.

'There are no peas,' she said, taking off her apron, folding it and placing it on the sideboard.

Walter looked up, expecting some explanation for why there were no peas. His mother sat down and took up one of the serving spoons. She placed it in the middle of the vegetables and aimed the handle towards Walter. Then she did the same with the casserole dish and waited for Walter to serve himself.

'No peas?'

'No,' she replied, as if the fact was of no consequence and needed no further explanation.

Walter was confused. Today was Tuesday. On Tuesdays they would have lamb casserole, served with potatoes, carrots and peas. She had been to the hairdressers, he could tell. The front of her hair had been coiffed into two semicircles either side of her forehead, and the hair on her crown seemed to have been fluffed up somehow. On her way back, she would have passed the Tesco Metro, and he was pretty sure that they had all sorts of peas in the frozen section: garden peas, petit pois, minted peas, Tesco's basic range peas.

He looked down at his plate and a sudden panic gripped him. His mother did not like going out in the dark, so if he wanted peas he would need to put on his coat and get them himself. It was a ten-minute walk. In the meantime, the rest of his meal would get cold. Perhaps his mother could put the food back in the saucepans and heat it up again? Or perhaps it would not take long if he ran? *Ran.* He dismissed the thought out of hand. In any case, if he went to get peas – two trips of ten minutes, ten minutes to cook them (unless his mother boiled the kettle while he was out so that they could go straight into hot water) – he would lose a total of thirty minutes. His carefully planned evening did not include an impromptu excursion to Tesco Metro to get frozen peas. Walter stared at his plate and tried to imagine the gap where the peas should be, filled with carrots and potatoes, with casserole gravy seeping in between.

'Alright?' his mother asked.

Walter thought, no, it's not all right. It's absolutely not all right. But there was nothing for it. A discussion would only take up more time. He reached for the vegetables.

'I saw Mrs Eardisley today,' said his mother, suddenly.

Walter's arm froze in mid-air. Was this an attempt to explain the train of events? Had his mother seen Mrs Eardisley and then forgotten to collect the peas?

'Oh?'

His mother gazed at his suspended arm but said nothing more. Walter served up his portions and then waited for his mother to do the same. They both picked up their cutlery.

'Her grandson's going to Cambridge to study maths.'

Walter felt his intestines sag. First the peas, now they were going to have the same old conversation about why he hadn't gone to Cambridge twenty-four years earlier. His fork hovered over a chunk of lamb as he calculated the additional wasted minutes if he rose to the challenge.

'Oh?' he replied, squeezing the tines of his fork into the square chunk.

They ate on in silence.

'Her grandson has been very single-minded, she says.'

Walter chopped a carrot into three equal-sized lengths, lined them up in front of his fork and pierced them simultaneously.

'Oh?'

'He wants to work at *Cern*, she says.'

'Does she?'

'*He. He* wants to work at *Cern*.'

'So *she* says.'

Walter was getting the distinct impression that his mother was trying to be annoying. First the peas, then this old business – harping on about things. Walter chopped up the remaining carrots. They were of unequal size and he found it disconcerting.

'I could have worked at Cern if I hadn't been born a woman. Women like me didn't stand a chance. We had no opportunity. Not the opportunities you've had. It's all about opportunity, isn't it? My primary school teacher told me that I was the best mathematics pupil he'd ever had. He more or less admitted that if I were a boy, I'd go far. If you're good at mathematics, you can do anything. The world's your oyster.'

'Arithmetic.'

'Sorry?'

'Arithmetic. You were good at arithmetic. Counting – adding and subtracting. Times tables. That kind of thing. Not mathematics.'

Gurda's fork, laden with half a potato, froze in mid-air and her mouth dropped open.

Walter cut a potato in two and ate one half. Normally, he would have left the topic there, hanging in mid-air like his mother's fork. But whether it was the peas that had annoyed him, or the flies at the bottom of the umbrella stand, he had a sudden urge to say exactly what was going through his head.

'You know, mother, it is quite wrong to call simple numerical manipulation "mathematics", when one should really refer to it simply as "arithmetic". Mathematics involves all kinds of disciplines such as geometry, calculus, trigonometry, algebra et cetera, et cetera. I would agree that it is impossible to be good at mathematics without first being good at arithmetic, but the fact that one is good at arithmetic does not mean that one is a gifted mathematician. It might interest you to know that the world's most eminent mathematicians were all highly creative people. Einstein could not have written his essay on mathematical proofs, using the Theorem of Menelaus, if he was merely a genius at arithmetic. In fact, wasn't it Einstein himself who said, "The true sign of intelligence is not knowledge but imagination"?'

'Imagination?' said his mother, eventually. 'There's no such thing as imagination in mathematics. Not unless you're talking about creative accounting. I was never involved in anything like that. The books at T. J. Morgan's were spotless, I can tell you. Can you imagine what the director would have said if he'd found anything "creative" in my accounts? I don't know what kind of mathematics they're encouraging you to teach at that school of yours.'

Walter mopped up the gravy with the last of his potatoes. It was impossible to have a coherent debate with someone who twisted what you were saying out of all recognition. He swirled the potato around until the plate was clean then laid down his knife and fork. It was a good thing he hadn't pursued the idea of getting more frozen peas. Glancing over his mother's head, he saw that it was nine minutes to six. He was about to take his plate to the sink when his mother added,

'If you hadn't wasted time being creative with that piano, you could have been anything. Your teachers all said you could have gone to Cambridge or Oxford or even America. You could have travelled the world.'

Walter stared at his plate. He realised that a thin ribbon of gravy had been left, meandering across the white glaze. It irked him that he had missed it in his eagerness to leave the table. He'd eaten everything so quickly there was nothing left to mop it up with. There might be a potato left in the saucepan, but that would mean getting up, serving it, probably having to offer something else to his mother in the process, prolonging the conversation. The gravy would have to stay. He grabbed his plate and rose from the table.

'Walter!' said his mother.

'What?'

'Not "what" – "pardon"!'

'Pardon?'

Walter waited. His mother seemed to be staring at

something peculiar on the wall. In any case, she was motionless for a moment then began to sway her head around as if the thing she'd been watching had suddenly taken flight and was flitting around her head.

'Oh, for goodness sake! Never mind!' She returned to her food and Walter saw her cut into a chunk of lamb with a great deal of unnecessary force. Perhaps she was also annoyed about the peas?

Walter went in to the kitchen and placed his plate in the sink. He turned and walked back through the dining room, along the hallway and right, into the front room. The orange street lamps cast a comforting light, and the black ebony veneer of the piano seemed to glow. He closed the door and without turning on the central light, he sidled around the piano. The room was small and although the piano was only a baby grand, it took up most of the space. The piano faced the door with the keyboard nearest the window. Bringing the curtains together, he made sure that they overlapped evenly and that there were no gaps. He hated the thought that anyone could see him playing. He bent down and switched on an anglepoise lamp that was perched on a pile of music books. *There.* Light flooded the keys.

Walter moved between the stool and the piano, sat down and sighed. On the wall facing him the sunburst clock, which had gold-coloured metal spikes radiating outwards from the pearly face, said two minutes to six. Perfect. He had negotiated all the day's hurdles and was finally sitting in the place he loved most in the world. He opened the lid. The cover of the book in front of him was yellowed with age, and the bottom corners of the pages were curled and brown. How was it possible for something so beautiful to be expressed in such an unremarkable way?

The orchestra, which in his mind had been tuning its violins, was ready. He was about to open the book's cover, when something held him back. Something was not quite right about the room. The piece was long. Once started, he wanted no distractions. Better deal with it now, whatever it was. Walter scanned the room. The light from the lamp was just right. The front room door was closed, to discourage interruptions. The curtains were perfect.

It was not something visual he realised; it was olfactory. He sniffed the air. There were the usual sitting room smells, furniture polish and potpourri. Perhaps the potpourri was going off? He sniffed his shirtsleeve. Perhaps it was him? The smell of sweaty children, chalk and felt pens? No, it was something else. The lingering smell of something burnt. Burnt food? Walter's heart sank. Burnt peas. He sniffed again. It was definitely burnt peas. He could visualise them clearly, brown and shrunken at the bottom of the pan, each individual pea leaving a ghostly brown shadow around it, like the imprint of a nuclear explosion. The saucepan would never be clean again. There would always be a mottled black pattern on the base. So that's where they went.

Walter checked the time on the clock. One minute past six. It was no use wasting more time thinking about the fate of the peas. Time was slipping away. But he did need to get rid of this awful smell. It was a major distraction. He couldn't concentrate on Rachmaninoff's third piano concerto whilst thinking about burnt peas.

He got up from the stool and reached behind the curtain for the window latch. He lifted it and slid it outward so that it caught on the slot. Immediately he felt the cool evening air on his wrists and caught the smell of traffic fumes. Traffic fumes were better than burnt peas he decided and turned to sit down.

The orchestra had tuned up for a second time. The musicians would be getting impatient. He sat but, even before he had a chance to raise his hands to the music, something brushed against his shoulders. Glancing behind him, he saw that the curtains were now billowing away from the window.

He stood and faced the window and just as he did so, the fabric parted around him. Car headlights blinded him. He felt as if he'd suddenly walked on to an enormous stage.

'This won't do,' he muttered, grabbing both curtains and pulling them tightly across so that they overlapped by several feet. But he knew as soon as he let go, they would billow again. *It's all her fault. If she hadn't burnt the peas I wouldn't have this problem. In fact, if it wasn't for her I wouldn't have most of my problems – billowing curtains, burnt peas, my awful job, THAT school.* An image of his father appeared to him, belting out of the door with his hat and coat flying. Surely, he was imagining that? Wouldn't he have been too young to remember? That was her fault too.

Walter groaned. He couldn't stand here all evening holding the curtains. He would either have to close the window and put up with the blasted smell or he would have to find a way to fasten the curtains together. He craned his neck around to look at the clock. He'd already wasted six minutes and hadn't played a single note.

Then, he remembered the horrible umbrella stand. He remembered the dead flies, and the paperclips. *That's it.* He would fish out the paperclips, avoiding the dead flies, and use them to hold the curtains together so that he could get on with his piano. He let go of the curtains. The thought of being exposed to the audience again was unnerving so he switched off the lamp and the room was bathed in an orange glow punctuated by sweeping headlights.

He went out into the hall and looked towards the kitchen. Thankfully, his mother had finished eating her dinner and was back in the kitchen out of sight. He could hear her washing the dishes. The radio was on.

He walked towards the front door and came to a stop by the umbrella stand. It really was peculiar. He placed his hands around it and lifted. It was heavier than it looked and he realised that he should have opened the front door before picking it up. He gathered the stand into his left arm and reached out to open the door with his right. Everything would soon be going according to plan. He pulled the door open then pushed it wide against the hallway wall. Two seconds and he would be back inside.

He stepped out into the chilly evening street. It was the height of rush hour, and the road was at its noisiest. There was a faint hint of fish and chips on the breeze. For a brief second he wondered whether mushy peas might have worked with the casserole. He hadn't thought of that.

He turned the stand over. It had corners and sharp edges everywhere and manoeuvring it was tricky. Small objects fell on to the path, and when he looked down he could see the three paperclips on the ground. They shone in the light, even though they seemed to have bits of fluff attached to them. The flies must have come out too, although he couldn't see them. He turned the stand upright and peered in. One fly had disappeared but the other, presumably caught on a cobweb, was suspended miraculously at the centre of the stand as if levitating.

Just as he was pondering the levitating fly and wondering how he could get it out without touching it, or whether indeed he would bother removing it at all, given that he had already wasted so much time, he heard a whooshing noise and an enormous slam as the door shut behind him in a gust of wind.

Damn.

A sheet of newspaper fluttered by on the street.

Now he would have to ring the bell which would bring his mother to the door which would result in a completely time-wasting conversation about why he was standing there, outside, holding the umbrella stand.

Surely she had heard the slam? The pea incident suggested she might be losing her marbles. Perhaps her hearing was going too? He waited a little longer. Nothing.

Holding the stand in the crook of his left arm, he reached out for the doorbell and pressed. Hardly anyone ever rang the doorbell so the sound was shockingly shrill and unexpected. Nevertheless, Walter held his finger on it for a good long while just to make sure that she'd heard.

He waited. Nothing.

'Oh, for goodness sake.' He pressed the bell again, longer this time.

'Walter!' he heard her shout. 'There's someone at the door!'

God. He closed his eyes.

He pressed the doorbell again and kept his finger on it.

Through the glass, Walter could see a shadow approaching. She was shouting something. The door opened and Walter took his finger off the bell. Gurda Wagstaff looked at her son, then at the stand, then at her son.

'What IS the matter with you? And what do you think you're doing with that?' she asked. Annoyingly, she had made no attempt to stand aside to let him in. He hated the way she forced him to answer questions that really did not warrant the time or effort to engage with.

'I was cleaning it out.'

He stepped towards her, but still she didn't move.

'I can promise you, there was no dust in there. I cleaned it out only the other day. I'm not too old to take the vacuum around you know. I suppose you're suggesting that... '

At which point, Walter decided that he really did need to get past her, back in to the sitting room, back to the piano and the rest of the evening which he had been looking forward to since last Friday. His mother was saying something, rather more loudly than she needed to. He considered telling her that he wasn't in the next street, but instead he squeezed past, entered the sitting room and closed the door firmly behind him.

Thank God. But his heart sank almost immediately. He

was holding the umbrella stand, which he didn't need, and the paperclips, which he did need, were still outside on the path. He put the stand on top of the piano and went back into the hall.

'... she was as straight as a poker at ninety-three and still going strong. No one would have dared suggest that she couldn't do her own cleaning. She used to walk into town on her own to fetch her shopping, always dressed to the nines, pearls and all... '

Walter was alarmed to find his mother standing in the same spot, apparently talking to herself. He would have asked her who she thought she was talking to, but really the evening was slipping away. He opened the front door as wide as he could, dashed out on to the path, peered for the three paperclips, found them and returned to the house, closing the door behind him.

'... respect their elders. After all we did in the war. Did we get any thanks? Our parents would never have dreamt of patronizing their superiors... '

Walter slammed the door to the sitting room. What a stupid place to put an umbrella stand was his first thought on seeing it perched on top of the piano. But the curtains were billowing around the piano stool. *Curtains first.*

Straightened out, the paperclips were surprisingly effective at holding curtains together. He spaced them evenly then stood back to survey his work. He reckoned that unless someone was an eight-foot giant, or a crouching midget, they would not be able to see a thing. He felt rather pleased with himself. He turned and sat at the piano. The clock on the wall said fourteen minutes past six. For once, the noise of traffic through the open window was strangely comforting. It was masking whatever his mother was saying. Inexplicably, she was still talking.

He opened the cover of the book to the first page. He picked up a white cloth, which was folded neatly to one side of the keyboard, and gave the keys a delicate wipe. He folded the cloth and replaced it, then rubbed his hands together and stretched his fingers. He extended his feet to the pedals and judged whether the distance was perfect. He moved the stool back a fraction. He sat upright, breathed deeply and let his shoulders relax. He sighed and felt a fleeting, unbearable sadness. Then he closed his eyes.

The strings and clarinet came in right on cue. Two notes, repeated. It was a short introduction. No long preamble. Walter brought up his hands and laid his fingers lightly on the keys. The beginning was simplicity itself. Five notes in a minor key. Everyone thought they could play Rachmaninoff's third when they heard the introduction. A child could play it. But he knew it was a lure, a sweet deception. He smiled. Now let's leave the novices behind, he thought, and the piece took flight. His hands moved over the keys like shallow waves over rippling sands. He felt his spirit soar. The theme dived beneath, like an undercurrent through deep water, ebbing, flowing. Now the notes were rivulets, rushing water funnelled between narrow channels. The accents were like jutting stones in the stream. Here and there, his hands stretched beyond octaves. He loved the feeling of expansion.

There was a pause in the piano section. The orchestra played on. He rested his hands on his lap and swayed with each phrase. He felt his lungs fill. The music raised him up to see vistas. Horizons stretched before him. Now it was his turn. He held his breath, it was so fragile. A floating melody, delicate as blossom on a breeze. But, sure enough, the low notes soon piled in on themselves. Here was the threat of a gale through a dense forest. His hands struggled to keep up. With each beat he rose up in his seat – new phrases came in. Two melodies were weaving through each other like banners caught in the wind.

The theme returned. This time, he felt his heart expand as the pace slowed for a moment. This was a time to breathe, to prepare. His head fell back. The orchestra took up the melody and played on without him for a moment. There were the clarinets and the oboes. In came the strings. It was exquisite. He could see the violinists, their bows moving in unison, breathing together, like some great creature. He joined them. It was deceptively simple like a great swell under a boat. But there he was again, Rachmaninoff, lulling him into a false sense of security. The calm didn't last. Now he was on a turbulent sea. There was lightening, thunder, whirlpools and spray.

And just as suddenly, the sky cleared. It was full of stars. In amongst them there was a single, icy star – brightest of all in the darkest sky. Walter marvelled at its crystal beauty. His hands were warm now. They flew over the keys with ease. He played playful running notes, like they were sparks. Here and there they dashed only to pause again. There were lonely horns in a stately funeral. Walter leant back and enjoyed another pause. Another lull, before a greater storm.

And here it was, unexpectedly, a third of the way through the concerto, the hardest part of all, not at the finale as everyone expected, but here. Here, now, this is where he needed to be brave, to hold his nerve. This is where the orchestra abandoned him. This is where there was nowhere for him to hide. The stage was his. All eyes were on him. The orchestra and the audience held their breath. He needed every ounce of strength. The music towered above him, Rachmaninoff's monumental design testing every sinew.

He was through. The notes fell away. In the stillness, a single flute joined him, then a clarinet, then a horn. And again he was abandoned by the orchestra but this time to such dropping notes, like raindrops making rings in a pool at dusk.

The orchestra returned, along with the theme. Its simplicity seemed sadder. It was intricate, like following the pattern in a piece of lace. The notes were here, there, he chased them. They tried to evade him, like quick rabbits they darted through undergrowth. Oh, but I'll catch you, thought Walter. I'll play you all, every one of you. He and the music were running together now, step for step.

Another pause, then a rill, a fast-flowing stream. There was water on leaves, endlessly pouring, catching the light, splashing, sparkling. A sudden drum's beat. He felt it in his bones. He wasn't thinking about his hands now. He was Rachmaninoff's messenger. He was just a vehicle. Perfection existed and all he had to do was find a way to make it come alive. The composer was with him in the room. Rachmaninoff was conducting and he, Walter, was playing. What a gift he'd been given.

There was a swirl and the scene changed. The skylark that had hovered above a sun-drenched field dived down. The ground shook. A startled mouse scurried away through the long grass. There was the sound of approaching hooves, of galloping horses. A chase. Jumps over rivers, a race along a high ridge, a march – an advancement. This is where it all came together. These were the notes he had worked so hard to reach, the phrasing he'd strained so hard to express. Now he needed all his strength, all his precision. The entire orchestra swelled behind him. Every instrument was playing its part. The music climbed, climbed as if to reach a peak on a snow-capped mountain. Walter was hunched over the keys now, concentrating, willing his hands to work quicker, to be stronger, more accurate so that the end would be as Rachmaninoff had designed it to be. He was approaching the finale now. Cymbals clashed. With the final triumphant notes his entire body sprang upwards – his hands flew into the air.

Bravo! The crowd leapt to its feet in ecstasy. They roared. *Bravo! Bravo!* They shouted. *Virtuoso!* It was incredible! Perfection! Even the orchestra was applauding him now. The conductor too, tapping his baton on the lectern.

Oh, it was perfect! Walter was exhausted. He stood and placed his hand on the edge of the piano to steady himself.

He let his head drop back, breathed, then dropped forward into a deep bow. He was wrung out. The crowd cheered. *Bravo! Bravo!* He stood up, then bowed again, even deeper. Walter could see the reviews. *Brilliant performance! The work of a true genius! Unprecedented technical skill!* He took another bow, turned to face the orchestra and clapped them too. The crowd went wild.

The cheers continued for a long time then eventually they began to fade. The sound receded like the sound of waves being drawn out on a gravelly shore. It became further and further away. He strained to hear it – to keep the sound in his head. Eventually, it was replaced by the familiar drone of traffic along Northern Avenue.

Walter returned to his seat. The book was still on page one. He smiled and wondered why he needed to have it there at all. He had learned the piece off by heart many years ago. The years since then had just been a process of perfecting. On Friday he would play it again, while his mother was at her reading group.

He looked at the clock. Two minutes to seven. He didn't want to return to the dining room just yet. He sighed and thought of that fateful concert all those years ago. His music teacher, Mr Oliver, had persuaded him to play a solo, knowing that he was one of the few children who took piano lessons outside school.

'Play something nice. You know, Mendelssohn's Songs Without Words, or something like that.' Walter could tell that the teacher thought he was taking a bit of a punt – never having heard him play.

So, perhaps it was a fit of teenage pique that led him to choose Rachmaninoff. Not the third, that time, but the more well-known second – the first ten pages. His mother told him that everyone knew it because of the film, *Brief Encounter*. Walter had no patience with films but figured that the audience would be more likely to listen if they were familiar with the tune. *Tune.* That was one word for it. He practised all term and when the evening came, his nerves almost overcame him. The teacher more or less shoved him on stage, between a third year's bizarre ventriloquist act and a fifth year's impersonation of Alvin Stardust in full sparkly costume. Walter's knees trembled as he crossed the stage and all he could think of as he sat down was that he'd forgotten to tell the teacher that the piece wouldn't be Mendelssohn's after all.

But as his fingers touched the keys the old magic happened. His nerves vanished. He felt light. The world closed in. There was only him and the keyboard, and the black dancing notes that lured him into the page. He was released into the music. He flew like a hunting hawk. He completely forgot to stop.

When he came to the end, he'd lost track of where he was. Even worse, the hall was entirely silent. He glanced at the audience. They were still there. Everyone had a slightly shocked look. What had happened? Perhaps he should have played the Mendelssohn after all? The spell was only broken when Mr Oliver crossed the stage, looking flushed and puffy around the eyes, clapping loudly. He was making his way towards Walter at speed. Walter got up quickly, thinking that the combination of speedy approach and loud clapping was a bad thing and that he should exit the stage as quickly as possible. In fact, he was already half way across when he felt the teacher grab him by the shoulder and pull him back. At which point, the audience started clapping. They clapped and clapped. Walter thought they'd never stop. Those at the front, including the Headmaster and his wife, the Deputy Head and her husband and some other people Walter didn't recognise, stood up. They were cheering wildly now. Walter wasn't sure why they were reacting that way. Everyone was smiling, or worse still, laughing. He didn't think he'd done anything funny. He hadn't tried to be funny. Not like the ventriloquist.

She'd been funny. In parts.

Walter tried to leave the stage but the teacher's grip on his shoulder was so firm he couldn't budge. *Bravo! Bravo!* Everyone shouted.

'Can I go now, Mr Oliver?'

'Enjoy it, Walter,' replied Mr Oliver, looking puffier than ever, 'it's your moment of glory!'

Walter looked back at the audience. Some of them looked crazed.

Eventually the teacher let go and after the concert finished, Walter had gone home to where his mother was waiting for him with a plate of beans and fish fingers. He had kept the concert a secret, and he was very pleased he had, given the raucous response.

And that was that, or so Walter thought, until he was called to the Headmaster's office the following week. He had good news. A letter. One of the children's parents had attended the concert. They were related to someone at a famous school of music. They had told them all about his Rachmaninoff. This person had spoken to the music teacher. The music teacher had spoken to the Headmaster. The Headmaster had spoken to the music school. A lot of people had been talking to each other.

The letter was an invitation to audition but, by the sounds of it, it was merely a formality. His performance had been outstanding. There was no doubt about it. The school had spotted his talent and were now jolly well going to make sure that he was given the opportunity he deserved.

'You're going to go far, Walter. Take this letter home to your parents. Have a chat with them. We'll take it from there.'

Walter wanted to explain that he didn't have 'parents' that, in fact, he only had one 'parent'. He didn't like to mislead people. But the Headmaster ushered him out to the sound of the school bell.

'What's all this?' his mother had asked, twisting her

mouth into an odd shape so that she exhaled cigarette smoke sideways through the open back door. She was going through a short-lived but deeply committed 'Twiggy' phase at the time, and this was somehow connected to taking up smoking.

'Have you been up to no good?' she said, tearing the letter open with her pink nails. 'I don't understand. Why would they want to send you to another school? I thought your marks were good? They're good in maths. I don't see the point, even if they are going to pay a – what do they call it – bursary? Would they do maths at this new school?' She read on. *A specialist music school. World-renowned.* That's like saying world-renowned cookery school or university for knitting. *Yehudi...* oh, I can't even say that. *Natural ability... creative ...*' His mother inhaled noisily. 'Don't you worry, Walter. I'll have a word with the Headmaster. I know you. You want to study mathematics, like I did. A proper subject that'll get you places. I can't see how music is going to get you anywhere – unless you were really brilliant, of course. But you'd have to be really brilliant like Pavarotti or, you know, Nureyev.'

'But...'

'Don't get me wrong, Walter. I think it's a great thing in itself. Look at Auntie Margaret. She loved playing that piano. I know that's partly because she never had a proper job, a nine to five job with a title – like the one I had – but she got such a lot of pleasure out of it. It's a great hobby, Walter, a fantastic thing to do in your spare time. Aunt Margaret held that church together. It would have shut in the 1960s without her. She was the best funeral organist for miles around... '

Walter had pretty much stopped listening by that point. His mother shoved the letter back in the envelope and slipped it behind the carriage clock on the sideboard.

'So what are we going to do about the music school, Walter?' the Headmaster would ask him when they passed in the corridor. But either the Headmaster forgot eventually or Walter's mother really did go to see him because in the end he stopped asking. Everything went back to normal. Apart from the fact that Walter vowed he would never play for an audience again. Once was enough. He was very pleased when everyone finally stopped asking him about it.

'Walter!' His mother shouted from the dining room. 'I hope you're not going to play that thing again. It's very stressful. All that banging and crashing. You always play it as if you're in such a rush! Think about the neighbours! Can't you play something a bit more relaxing? How about some nice Elton John?'

Walter closed the music book. In the distance he could hear a siren. They came by so often he hardly heard them now. He looked at the clock. It was five minutes past seven. Time to mark work for the following day. He wondered why it was that he had heard his mother so clearly. Then it struck him that the traffic noise had stopped. He stood up and teased open the curtain between the paperclips. The junction was a sea of cars. They all seemed to have their headlamps on but they had come to a standstill. Some were idling quietly but most had switched off their engines. Some of the car doors were open and their drivers had got out. What on earth were they thinking? Surely it was dangerous to stop in the middle of a major junction? In the far distance, as far out as the motorway, he could see blue lights weaving their way through stationary traffic.

Walter looked back at the junction. It was only now, as his eyes became more accustomed to the glaring headlights, that he could see what had stopped them. Right next to the traffic lights there was an upturned van wedged against a lamp post, and in the foreground, a group of people crouched near the ground. They appeared to be gathered around a mangled bike. Someone was lying on the tarmac. That someone was wearing a jacket just like the one Dean Bayliss had been wearing.

Walter shut his eyes and brought the curtain edges

together again as quickly as he could. He'd had enough distractions for one evening – what with the awkward cleaner, the burnt peas and his demented mother. Whatever was going on outside was definitely nothing to do with him. All he wanted was to be left alone. Was that too much to ask? He wasn't bothering anyone. He was perfectly happy just going about his life, minding his own business. Ainge Terrace was perfect for that. No one in their right mind wanted to stop here. That suited him just fine.

With his eyes still shut, he reached behind the fabric and fumbled for the window latch. After a few awkward adjustments the latch finally aligned itself with the upright pin and it fell into place with a screech. What a relief. Now he could safely remove the paperclips without worrying about the billowing curtains. He opened his eyes and removed each one in turn. Thank goodness there were no obvious holes even though the fabric was quite thin. He turned to look at the time. Fifteen minutes past seven. He calculated thirty-five minutes to mark test papers then another twenty-five minutes to write his homework plans for the following day. Ten minutes to heat up and drink his warm milk. Tomorrow was Wednesday. Only another three days before he could play the piece again.

What a stupid place to put an umbrella stand, he thought, fleetingly, then remembered the train of events. No doubt the fly was still in there, suspended by some invisible cobweb. What on earth made it want to die in there, he wondered? He felt sad for the fly that it had ended its days in a hideous umbrella stand, sort of levitating, out of sight, not really doing the sorts of things flies were designed to do. He turned to switch off the lamp and realised that it was already off. How funny. He had played the entire piece by the glow of the orange street lamps. Given that there was enough light to see, it was strange that it had never occurred to him before. All that unnecessary switching on and off of lights. All those wasted minutes. Added up, they could make quite a difference.

He closed the piano lid gently and made his way towards the door, picking up the umbrella stand as he went.

AT A JUNCTION

There was a horrible, rubbery screech and Emil Stein, concert pianist, was catapulted forward so hard that he ended up being pasted against the back of the driver's seat like a splatted cartoon cat.

'Oh, my giddy aunt!' said the driver, Gregory, once he'd wrestled the car to a stop.

Emil was just peeling himself off the plush black leather when another car flew past them, taking out a bollard. It came to an ungainly stop, perched on top of it. A second screech, behind them this time, was followed by a delicate, almost musical release of broken glass. There was a bump, and their car was shunted forward, narrowly missing the one in front.

'Bloody hell,' said Gregory. He wasn't normally one to swear. 'Did you see that?'

Emil had been too busy checking his recital schedule to notice anything going on in the outside world. 'What happened?' he asked, sweeping his wavy blonde hair back over his forehead. Through the clouds of dust and smoke, and the sickly glow of orange street lamps, he could see that a van had somersaulted on to the central barrier, wedging itself up against a lamp post and something that looked like a hanging basket.

'A lad on a bike, came out of nowhere – came right across... what a mess!'

Emil looked around and tried to work out where they were. Some dog-eared part of the city, by the look of it. They appeared to have stopped in the centre of a huge five-way junction, with traffic lights in every direction.

'You stay here,' said Gregory, 'I'm going to take a look.'

They both knew Emil wouldn't be venturing out himself.

Not that people were likely to recognise him. People didn't generally recognise him, thought Emil. But that was more a reflection on their level of education or lack of musical taste rather than how famous he was. Besides, the car windows were blacked out, thank goodness. And in any case, he had plenty to do while the road was being cleared. Emil craned his neck to see if he could spot Gregory. He couldn't. There were a lot of people running around. He wasn't sure what they were doing.

Emil's diary and paperwork had slipped and scattered in the sudden stop. He leant forward to pick them up. He put the loose papers on the seat next to him then turned his attention to the pages in his diary. Earlier on, his PA had told him about a last minute invitation to play in Stockholm. *Stockholm in January! I don't think so.* This time last year he'd been performing at an amazing festival in Rio de Janeiro. Now that had been worth the flight. It was a new development for him – South America. The audiences had been very appreciative and surprisingly knowledgeable. He flicked through the weeks ahead: Lucerne, Boston, Vienna – such a stunning auditorium, Berlin, Paris – the best venues in the world. He swiftly passed over the words 'Carnegie Hall!!' which had an impatient thick line drawn through them. Carnegie wasn't the best auditorium by a long chalk, but he had always had a hankering to play there. Being passed over for a younger, 'more marketable' female pianist still rankled. She wasn't exactly playing fair either. When she performed she seemed to wear less on stage than most women he knew wore to bed. His team was still working on it, though. Although, he was damned if he was going to turn up in a backless shirt or trousers cut down to his bum.

'But look,' he'd reminded the team, 'I'm not desperate. Only if it fits with my schedule. I've got to work around all my charity stuff and there's Jeremy's holidays to consider, don't forget.'

Jeremy. He hadn't seen him for weeks. He would be getting pretty grumpy by now. *Mental note: ask the PA to order a consignment of that hideously expensive cologne.*

Emil looked over the passenger headrest to see whether there was any progress on the road. Everything seemed to have gone very quiet. He scanned the sad looking Victorian terraces. The people up front could have chosen a more scenic place to have an accident. The street lamps made the scene look garish, like a man in drag. But, to be fair, the city's concert hall had been rather impressive. It was still new and a little shiny, and had none of the gravitas of the more established venues. But it had a promising feel about it. Nicely placed on the harbour. A smartly dressed audience. He liked that. He liked to think that people made the effort. It was a mark of respect for him, and for his art. He had no patience with these people who turned up in jeans, looking like they'd been dragged through a hedge backwards. Even less patience with musicians who did the same, expecting audiences to take them seriously. It was laughable really. Would the prime minister turn up to work in a set of overalls? And the Queen – now there was a smart lady. He'd been introduced to her at the South Bank. No flies on her.

Emil set the diary down on the seat next to him and picked up the pile of paperwork. It was a jumbled mess of performance notes and press releases. There was fan mail too, but only a small sample. His team must have selected the most interesting ones rather than waste his time. He flicked through them: *Stunning. Delightful. Exquisite. Pleasing.* Pleasing? Emil re-read the sentence. 'Your rendition of Beethoven's piano concerto number five was very pleasing, and although not as eloquent as Kaspar Volkov's performance, which we saw in Sydney last year, it was nonetheless masterfully done.'

Pleasing! In the same breath as Volkov! Emil tossed the letter aside and peered over the top of the passenger seat.

Oh, hurry up, will you?

Gregory had left the driver's door open and there was strong smell of traffic fumes. People's engines were still running. That was a good sign at least. It meant that they weren't going to be there long. Mingled with the fumes was the faintest smell of fish and chips. *Fish and chips and mushy peas.* He quite fancied that. Jeremy wasn't there to tell him off with his acerbic macrobiotic, vegan-cum-gluten-free guilt trip. Perhaps Gregory could do a detour once they'd got moving? He was from around here, wasn't he? This was his patch?

Then in the space of three minutes, a police car, a police motorbike and an ambulance turned up. Everything was a swirling cacophony of flashing blue lights and sirens. There was a lot of activity up ahead, and some of the drivers returned to their cars. A police officer was weaving his way between the vehicles, updating people on progress. He peered in through the open door.

'Alright, mate, where's your driver?'

Emil's mouth dropped open. There was so much wrong with that sentence. But before he could think of a clever riposte, the policeman added, 'You can't leave a car unattended with the engine running you know,' and to Emil's horror, he leapt in to the driver's seat.

'What have we got here, then? BMW, seven series. Nice. Let's put it out of action for a bit, shall we?' The officer made sure the handbrake was on and then switched off the engine.

He removed the keys from the ignition and tossed them back over his shoulder towards Emil.

'Don't want anyone kidnapping you, do we?'

Emil was pretty sure that the officer had absolutely no idea who he was, so could only assume that the comment was some kind of policeman-y joke. The officer got out of the car.

'We're not going to be here long, are we, officer?' asked Emil in the most obsequious tone he could muster. The officer sighed and leant back in through the open door.

'Mate, we have a distressed teenager who seems to have broken most of the bones in his legs, and who is currently depositing a significant percentage of his blood supply on the central reservation. Not to mention a bloke who's cleverly got himself pinned between his steering wheel, a lamp post and a hanging basket – although that doesn't appear to have diminished his ability to put the world and the entire police force to rights. The traffic's already backed up as far as the city centre. So you may be here quite a while. But don't worry. If you're stuck any longer than two hours we'll bring you some bottled water.'

Two hours! Emil watched the officer as he sauntered off towards the other cars. Nice arse he thought, resentfully. But the man was clearly a bit of a joker.

Emil groaned. Why did he have to spend so much of his life feeling like a prisoner? Blacked out cars, empty hotel rooms, private hire cars. It was one of the reasons he liked coming to Cardiff. He always used Gregory's company and it was great to see a friendly face. He and Gregory had chats about all sorts of things. Cooking, gardening, novels. He was a very nice man. Emil had even met his wife Marjorie. She was very sweet.

One by one the engines became silent. There was a brief flurry of excitement as the fire engine arrived – presumably to extricate the van driver from the hanging basket – and then everything became even quieter. Emil drummed his fingers along the top of the seat in front. He couldn't even hear distant traffic. They should have been on the M4 by now, speeding their way back to London. He had three days at the Kensington flat and then he was off to Ghent. *Ghent? Who's idea was that?* He couldn't remember agreeing to sodding Ghent. Still, it was a nice enough place. *Mental note: check with the team that they haven't put in that grim dog-hole of a place like last time.*

He rubbed his hands together. It was getting chilly.

Perhaps he could risk getting out and shutting the driver's door? He was hardly likely to be bombarded by autograph requests just here, was he? Massaging the joints in his right hand, he thought they felt a little sore. The Prokofiev always took it out of him. And it was getting windy. A sheet of newspaper fluttered by along the pavement. He could really murder a bag of fish and chips.

Just then, he caught the sound of something on the breeze. Two notes. D flat, D major, repeated for three bars. He recognised them immediately – the beginning of 'Rach Three'. He wished Gregory had left the radio on so that he could listen to something too. It would help to pass the time. He wondered if he could reach forward to the front of the car and switch it on, but he had no idea how the system worked. He would probably have to turn on the ignition. Knowing his luck he would probably set off the alarm. For a moment he toyed with the idea of creating enough disturbance to attract that police officer back. Wasting police time. Public disturbance. Maybe not.

He heard the music again, clearer this time. It was definitely the 'Rach Three'. For a long time he had considered adding it to his official repertoire. It was fiendishly difficult. People's reputations had been made or broken by it. He had vowed not to perform it until it was utterly perfect. After all, Volkov had tried it, and look where that got him. A promising start then, *quelle catastrophe*. Every now and again, usually when he and Jeremy were on holiday at their villa in Cap Ferrat, he would return to it. He could play it, but there was something about it that was completely unnerving. It was like a beautiful shoe that didn't fit. He knew it was a thing of beauty but invariably it caused him pain. He and Jeremy had come back early from the villa that time precisely because of it. Emil had been practising for hours every day, getting increasingly dispirited, and Jeremy had been particularly unsympathetic.

'Perhaps it's just not your thing,' he'd said, flicking the

latest Christie's auction catalogue in his direction. 'There are plenty of other amazing pieces. Why do get so worked up?'

Emil had tried explaining but it was no use. Jeremy was decorating again. There were 'mood boards' all over the place, which pretty much summed it all up, in Emil's opinion. Predictably, they'd ended up having a hellish row and got the PA to book return flights for that very evening.

Emil strained to hear the music through the open door. He wondered who the recording was by. They were good, whoever they were. Ashkenazy perhaps? No, it didn't sound like him. The music seemed to be coming from a terrace of miserable looking 1960s' houses to his right. What an architectural abomination, he thought. There was a window open on one of the oddly shaped bays. Some people have no idea about interior design, though Emil, looking at the untidy configuration of curtains. Despite all his quirks, he was lucky to have Jeremy. He really did know how to create a lovely environment.

Emil concentrated on the music. The recording was intriguing. He didn't recognise the style, but it was quite lovely. *Mental note: ask the team if there have been any recent recordings.* Maybe *Deutsche Grammophon* had released something new without sending him a copy? He found himself tapping his feet to the repeated theme.

There was a pause for the piano section. The clarinet entered along with the strings. It was exquisite. Then he realised that he knew the piece so well, he was imagining the orchestra. All was, in fact, silent. Perhaps he had imagined the whole thing? Then, perfectly on cue, the piano tumbled back in, like a waterfall of notes dashing themselves on to the intricate rocks of a cliff.

No orchestra? Who on earth would record without an orchestra? Emil sat up and stared at the row of peculiar houses. The sound was definitely coming from that one with the open window and the bizarre curtains. He listened. It was masterful – and at such a pace! Only Rachmaninoff himself played with that kind of speed. A remastered recording? Without an orchestra?

The music continued. It was technically perfect, which was a gargantuan feat in itself. But, oh, there was so much more to it than that. Listening to it was like looking at a vast landscape – if you stood back you could see it in all its immense majesty. Then, here and there, the playing drew you right in to the detail, to the living, breathing heart of it. It was tiny and exquisite. It was monumental and astonishing.

The theme returned again. Emil knew there was no orchestra, yet the pianist was making him hear it – somehow. How? It was extraordinary. Now the horn weaved its way through the theme along with the strings – they drew together, then parted. A drum roll, a simple series of notes – so easy to misjudge. Another pause, a playful interlude, and a sudden charge, like a storm breaking. The piano was an orchestra in itself. There seemed to be half a dozen melodies all playing at once.

He was transfixed. Whoever was playing was a master. How could the sound be coming from that tiny, miserable rabbit hutch? He sat forward and squeezed his eyes shut. He planted his forehead against the back of the seat and concentrated. It was breathtaking.

Eventually they came to the finale. Emil ran through all the recordings he had ever heard. No one had this skill – the delicacy, the nerve, the colour, the guts. It was spellbinding. He pressed himself against the car door. It was beyond perfection. It was transcendent. It was joy and delicious pain rolled together – the joy of hearing something so beautiful and the crushing realisation that such art was utterly out of his reach. He could never, ever, in a million years play the piece like that. He was in awe. He was transformed. He was utterly alive in the world. *Oh my God!* He was in love! It was a *coup de foudre! Bravo! Bravo! Bravo!*

He also wanted to die. Emil shoved open the car door and made a beeline towards the odd-looking row of houses. He swept his fingers through his hair. So what if someone recognised him. He had to know. It had to be some old recording, surely? He would find out. He would get his hands on a copy and study it. There might yet be a way to learn from this virtuoso. This genius. He could feel his heart thudding as he walked up the path and pressed his finger firmly on the doorbell. It made a hideous, shrill sound. *F sharp.* There was a light inside the house, but no movement. He knew he hadn't imagined it. He was quite certain it had come from this house. He drummed his fingers against his thigh. He could still hear it in his head. *Oh, God, don't let it fade.* He wanted to lie in its majesty, bathe in its glory.

Nothing happened. He pressed the doorbell again. *Where are you?* He was about to press the bell a third time when he heard a woman's voice from the interior.

'You can stay outside! I'm not playing any more of your silly games!'

Emil turned around. He was the only one at the door and he wasn't playing any games. Whoever they were, he wished they'd let him in. He was feeling rather on show, standing there, not getting any response. *Come on, come on.* He tried the doorbell again. He looked at the letter box and considered shouting through it. But then a shadow appeared in the hallway from the direction of the room with the window. It lingered, then seemed to reverse and slither backwards out of sight.

Emil went to the bay window and tried to see in through the curtains. The window that had been open earlier was now shut. It was all very odd. He couldn't believe that anything so exquisite could have emanated from such a dump, but he knew what he'd heard. He wasn't going mad. Emil pressed his nose up against the glass. There was a tiny gap where the curtains didn't quite meet. He squinted and wondered whether he should knock on the window, or whether that would be a little rude. Once his eyes adjusted to the light he saw the top of an anglepoise lamp. He twisted his head around to get a better look. There was sudden movement and then, without warning, an eyeball appeared in the gap. Emil sprang back.

He returned to the doorbell, pressed it again and held his finger there. *I know you're in there.* The doorbell screamed horrifically, then after a few moments it was joined, by means of accompaniment almost, by a woman shouting. It was difficult to make it all out. There was something about childish behaviour, a mathematics degree and frozen peas. This time the elusive shadow – which was connected, Emil presumed, to the alarming eyeball – returned at speed to the front door.

The man who opened the door was quite small, around five foot tall, mostly slim but with a little pot belly. He had very little hair, but what he had was a fair sandy colour and it was making a valiant effort to cover the top of his head. But in Emil's opinion, the most striking thing about this man was how angry he looked.

'Yes?' he hissed, as the door opened.

'My apologies for disturbing you… '

'Yes!'

'Yes?'

'You have definitely disturbed me!'

'I'm sorry. I don't like to impose, but would you mind giving me the details of that recording?'

Now the man looked more terrified than angry. He was dressed formally and neatly in suit trousers, white shirt and functional navy tie.

'We don't have any recordings here,' replied the man. Then to Emil's surprise, he began to close the door. No door had been closed in Emil's face for a very long time.

'The music,' said Emil placing his hand forcefully on the

door frame, 'the Rachmaninoff, if you please – all I want is the name of the pianist! If it's not too much trouble, I would be very grateful!'

The little man's response was to push harder against the door, and Emil was embarrassed to find himself responding likewise.

'I just want the name! I heard it with my own ears. It won't take a moment – who was it?'

'You've made a mistake. There are no recordings here. Go away.'

Emil protested. He explained that the traffic had come to a standstill because of the accident, and he had heard it quite clearly. There had been no doubt about it. Emil pushed as hard as he could but the little man was stronger than he appeared because he was putting up a good show and the door was closing.

In desperation, Emil gasped, 'It wasn't just me! We all heard it! All the people sitting in the cars heard it. We want to know who is in the recording!'

The little man faltered and through the gap in the doorway, Emil could see him glancing past him, scanning the cars, making a mental calculation of how many strangers were likely to bombard his front door.

Seeing his chance, Emil added, 'In fact, if you don't give us the details, we'll all be at your door, all one hundred and fifty three of us. We just want the name!'

This specific number clearly made an impression on the man because after a pause, he stepped back from the door. The fingers of his right hand fluttered nervously to his forehead, and he pushed away an imaginary strand of hair with a little backward flick of his head.

'Oh, dear,' he said.

'Look, I promise you, they won't come in. I just need the name of the pianist. Then I'll leave you in peace.'

'Oh, dear me,' said the man, and he stood aside to let

him in, closing the door firmly behind him.

Emil entered the sitting room but no sooner had he gone through the door than he realised that most of the room was taken up by an ebony baby grand. Unless the sound system was hiding under the piano, he couldn't see how there space for anything else in there. There was a lingering smell of cooked vegetables, and for some bizarre reason a large brass umbrella stand had been placed on top of the piano. He sidled around the room as far as the bay window. The curtains were creased and hanging untidily. Near the keyboard there were three misshapen paperclips. But apart from that, the room was clean and neat. He stood behind the piano stool and felt a shudder as if the tremor of an earthquake had moved through the room. On the stand in front of him was a copy of Rachmaninoff's third piano concerto.

'So, you see... ' said the man, fiddling with the imaginary strand of hair, 'No recording.'

Emil stared at the sheet music.

'Do you mind?' he asked, gesturing to the stool. The little man flicked his head in that haughty manner of his. Emil wasn't sure whether this meant it was alright to sit or not, but as his legs were giving way in any case, he presumed to sit.

'What's your name?'

'I don't see why that's... '

'What's your name?'

'Mr Wagstaff. But I really don't see what... '

'Do you know who I am?'

This man, Mr Wagstaff, didn't need to reply. It was clear from his response that he had no idea. Emil thought he'd tell him all the same.

'I am Emil Stein – concert pianist.' The man's face did not alter. 'At the moment, I believe I am ranked ninth amongst the world's most successful pianists. Some highly eminent critics would have me placed much higher – but whatever. I am up there – among the best, the highest paid classical musicians in the world. I have houses in Paris, Geneva, the Hamptons… '

The little man's attention was wavering. His eyes flickered to the window and back, then to a hideous sunburst clock on the wall.

'What I mean to say,' continued Emil, 'is that I know something about this piece. I know how it is supposed to sound.'

The little man's attention returned to Emil.

'I play for my own amusement. I am not trying to impress anyone.'

'Who taught you?'

'No one.'

'Who?' said Emil, a little more aggressively than he had intended.

'Well, Aunt Margaret, if you must know. Not any more, obviously. She died and gave me the piano. I did Grade III.'

Emil couldn't help it. He began to chuckle. At least it started as a chuckle. It was a strange kind of convulsive attack that took over his whole body until it began hurting his diaphragm. Then, what started as a release of tension, turned into a sob and tears began streaming down his face. He could sense Mr Wagstaff looking at him with distaste. The man must have been disturbed by the whole turn of events because he started to babble.

'I practise every Tuesday and Friday, mostly Fridays because my mother goes out to the film club that night. Or bingo. Mostly film club. Usually, I don't disturb anyone. It's certainly not my intention. That neighbour is deaf,' he said, pointing to one side of the room, 'and that one,' he said, pointing to the opposite side, 'is hardly ever at home. Apart from the traffic lights, it's very unusual for the traffic to be stationary out there. Very unusual indeed. In fact, this evening is the first time it's happened in twenty-two and a half years. No one stops at Ainge Terrace, not unless they want a parking ticket. Not unless they're mad. There are double yellow lines – everywhere.'

A tectonic plate was shifting underneath Emil's feet. He placed his hand on the piano's glossy veneer to steady himself.

'Please don't touch the piano,' said the little man.

Emil wiped his face with the back of his hand. 'I promise, I'll go away.'

'Good.'

'Only…' whispered Emil, 'I need to hear the piece once again. Then I really will go.'

Mr Wagstaff glanced at the curtains and sighed.

'I promise they won't come in.'

By the time Gregory returned to the car, Emil was already slumped in the back seat. He'd thrown the paperwork and diary aside and was dialling the PA.

Someone answered.

'Hello?' said Emil.

There was a response, but they were obviously in a busy place because they were having trouble hearing him.

'Can you hear me?' asked Emil. 'Listen. I don't want you to arrange any more venues. No. No more venues. Yes, I'm absolutely sure. No – no, not even the Carnegie.' There was a lot of hysterical screaming in the background. Emil hated having to repeat himself. 'The Car-ne-gie! Oh, it doesn't matter. If they want me, they can always come back.' There were more incoherent noises on the end of the phone and Emil only caught the last word. Fine?

'Yes, of course I'm fine. Well, we're stuck in a traffic jam as it happens, but otherwise, I'm fine. No, of course not. No, I didn't say anything about retirement. Who mentioned retirement? I'll decide about retirement when I'm good and ready.' There was a burst of laughter somewhere. He really wished his team was a bit more mature. Did they have to get so thoroughly plastered every Friday night?

'I can't hear you! Phone me in the morning! *Not* before eleven!'

Emil hung up and slumped back in his seat. Telling Jeremy was not going to be so easy. He was pretty sure he'd ordered a new car. Something low and shouty in electric blue. He leaned to his left and tried to see if anything was happening up ahead. Everything was very quiet now and although there were flashing lights, the sirens had been switched off.

Gregory was back in the driver's seat.

'All done?' Emil asked.

If Gregory did reply, Emil didn't hear it. Perhaps I'm going deaf he thought, feeling slightly aggrieved. 'Are they off to hospital?'

Gregory made a noise of some sort but it was incomprehensible and just as he was about to ask why they were still being held up the driver added, 'Poor bugger. Kept saying he could hear angels. Delirious I expect.'

'The van driver? The hanging basket?' ventured Emil, desperately trying to remember the policeman's words.

'Oh, no. He's alright, the chopsy bugger. Couple of broken ribs.'

'Oh, good. Well, not good, but… you know. Not dead.'

Gregory made an odd sound. Something halfway between a grunt of frustration and a groan of disbelief.

Up ahead, there was movement. An ambulance was driving off slowly, its lights flashing but no siren.

'Looks like we're moving,' said Emil. He'd had enough of this junction. So had Gregory by the looks of it, because he was slumped forward, cradling his head with his forearms.

'Fourteen… with a new bike,' said Gregory, his voice muffled by his jacket sleeves.

Emil was thinking of a response to his driver's cryptic comment when his phone pinged. A text from his team. 'Kaaaaarnnnneeeeeegeeeee!!' it said, followed by a series of silly faces making weird facial expressions. Emil tossed the phone aside in disgust and looked out of his window. Everything was starting to move, thank God. It was also starting to rain. The light from the lurid orange street lamps fragmented into a million shards as raindrops fell on the windscreen. Each drop of water clung desperately to the glass here and there until other bigger droplets ran into them. Emil watched as they streamed and collided at random.

Emil sighed. He had imagined that the end would come in a blaze of television appearances, lifetime contribution awards and retrospective specials on Channel 4. He thought it would be like a slow climb to a magnificent crest from where he would be able to look down with pride on a lifetime's achievement. There would be applause, plenty of it, and deep heartfelt bows. Tearful kisses blown to the balconies, huge bouquets. Large blousy peonies. Months of standing ovations. His name would be etched on granite plaques strategically located in smart public places. He would be embedded forever in the world's consciousness, like Julius Caesar and Einstein and Elvis.

But he'd been kidding himself. He could see that now. His career had been stuttering, like a candle that had been burning too long, the wick slowly drowning in its own molten pool. This is where it really ends, thought Emil, the whole bally shoot. It ends on an ugly junction in some random town.

He watched the raindrops on their giddy downward paths, veering from side to side, slowing now, then rushing on. They made him think of Rachmaninoff's beautiful tumbling notes.

The car moved off. Emil reached for his phone and switched it off. When was the last time he'd done that, he wondered? He leant back against the headrest and closed his eyes. Eventually, he fell asleep.

INDEPENDENCE DAY

He had been there for five months, three days and two and a half hours when he decided, not without some degree of provocation in his opinion, that the budgie's days were numbered. For most of his eighty-three years, Mansell Thomas had barely been aware of the existence of budgies, in the more general sense. He knew little more than they were greenish, lemon-yellowish sorts of birds that weren't native. He had a vague recollection of reading stories of how they had been used, many years before, as rudimentary early warning systems in coal mines. Something to do with gas? Later, he had heard stories of how some had escaped captivity and were terrorising inner cities. Or was that parakeets? More to the point, when he first moved to Llys-y-Fedwen nursing home, he had hardly noticed the large wiry construction in the far corner of the day room at all, or its pair of inhabitants. The occasional tweet that emanated from its bars had been fairly benign. The budgies had been happy then. All that had changed on the morning of the third of July when one of the budgies dropped dead.

With the benefit of hindsight, Mansell Thomas could swear that he had actually heard the feathered thing fall from its perch in the top-of-the-range *Liberté* bird cage, bumping into the faux rainforest branches twice on the way down. He realised afterwards that there had been a strange, unaccountable lull as if everything in the day room had paused momentarily. Totally coincidentally, the din of the 'nursery' music CD had come to an end, and the 'carer' (a misnomer if ever there was one in the opinion of Mansell Thomas) had stood stock-still. Her task every Tuesday morning was to throw exercise balls at the inmates in order to keep them alert. There had been a blissful moment of serenity. That's when one of the budgies, the remaining live budgie as it turned out, let out an almighty, blood-curdling squawk.

'Oh, my God!' said one of the women, pausing her Zimmer frame to peer with disgust at the bottom of the cage. 'One of the budgies has conked out.' Every member of the on-duty staff turned up at the day room to discuss the delicate issue of how to remove the dead body without allowing the remaining live one to escape. There were conflicting opinions regarding possible viruses, bird flu, notifiable diseases, whether the authorities should be informed or the vet called to attend to the distressed bird-widow.

Really, everything had kicked off from that point, and by five o'clock that evening Mansell Thomas had decided that the grieving budgie had to go. The question was, how? How to dispose of the remaining raucous creature without the act being traced back to him? He ate his supper in silence and lay in bed that evening pondering the question.

The following day, workmen arrived. The drains were being excavated ahead of a new extension and the garden was temporarily out of bounds.

'Can't be having you falling down any six-foot holes now can we?' laughed the Head Jailer, and Mansell thought the comment a tad indelicate given the subterranean look on some of the other inmates' faces. The workmen's luminous yellow safety vests seemed to be winding the budgie up. It was jumping from perch to perch and crashing, kamikaze-like into the sides of the wire cage. 'Someone should put it out of its misery,' muttered Mansell. He thought of the miners and wondered whether the budgie had turned into an early warning system for his own sanity. I wish someone would put me out of my misery, he thought.

Then later that morning, through an open window, Mansell heard part of a conversation.

'We've disturbed them,' said one of the builders.

'No worries,' said the other. 'We'll put down some rat

poison this afternoon.' They don't even try to pretend to be nice to pensioners these days, thought Mansell. Then his train of thought caught up with the situation and it came to him in a flash that he had found his solution. He stared at the bird. You won't be making that racket much longer, he thought.

After another meal – was it lunch or tea? – they were all much the same, Mansell went back to his room to 'get his book'. He'd been 'reading his book' for the last five months and two days. The bookmark had hardly moved but it was a convenient way of avoiding inane conversations with people who had forgotten their own names. He had never been a man to read. He was a 'doing' kind of man who liked to be out of doors. All this thinking was doing him no end of harm. Dwelling on things.

On the way back, he checked the corridor for staff. They were all on their tea break. Through the window he could see some of the builders sitting in the van with their feet wedged against the dashboard. Another dangled his legs out of the side. They all seemed to be glued to their mobile phones. Mansell pushed open the patio door and emerged into daylight. He couldn't remember the last time he'd been outside. The air was fresh and somewhere, not too far away, a neighbouring farmer must have been spreading muck. He felt a pang of sadness and wished he could be the one on the tractor.

He looked around at the builders' excavations, the exposed old drains and the piles of new plastic piping stacked on the side. He wondered whether rat technology had moved on so far that he wouldn't recognise the modern stuff? He bent down and peered into one of the open drains. Any moment now, he was expecting a shout from the van. 'Don't be overdoing it, grandpa!'

When he saw them, there was no mistaking the bright blue blocks stuffed inside an old Victorian pipe. Mansell glanced at the lads in the van then back through the windows behind him. The coast was clear. He took out his handkerchief, rubbed his nose for dramatic effect then dropped the hanky nonchalantly so that it fell near the pipe. He put all his weight on his less dodgy hip and poked the walking stick into the pipe, drawing the blue block and the fallen hanky towards him.

'Now then, Mr Thomas, what are we doing out here? Not making a run for it are we?' said the Head Jailer. You don't know the half of it, thought Mansell, bending forward. A fiery pain shot through his leg but as he straightened up, holding the lethal block hidden inside the handkerchief, Mansell thought it was well worth the agony.

'Good to see we've been doing our physiotherapy, Mr Thomas – well done!' We haven't been doing anything of the sort, thought Mansell. The hanky with its hidden block disappeared into his jacket pocket and he was ushered back inside. It smells of old people he thought resentfully, and couldn't quite believe that this is where he'd ended up. They'd got it all wrong in the Bible. You get born, you live, you get old, they put you in hell and then you die. Hopefully there was nothing after that apart from relief and a bloody long sleep. And some peace and quiet. That's what he was looking forward to most. The blue block in his pocket was going to help him deal with one irritation.

After supper, they all sat in front of the telly. Some young woman with hardly any clothes on was wailing pitifully in a kind of musical contest. The judges were making a meal out of their adjudication and Mansell wondered why they couldn't just tell her honestly and politely that she couldn't sing. *You sound like a bloody parakeet.* Perhaps a blue block would be a blessing for her family too?

Mansell felt for the lump in his pocket and hoped it wouldn't melt into the fabric. Was it possible to poison oneself with one's own jacket, he wondered? That would be a bit of an own goal. He had to remember to wash his hands carefully before going to bed. After he'd laid the poison of course. Mansell had concocted his plan. He'd kept back a chunk of that afternoon's lemon drizzle cake, helpfully baked by the local WI. While he was in the bathroom he'd rolled the sponge into tiny balls and hidden some poison inside. The lemon drizzle balls looked innocuous enough. He would pop them into the budgie's cage on the way to bed. No one would be any the wiser and by the morning the place would be a haven of tranquillity.

Eventually, it was time for bed. The staff began to usher the less mobile inhabitants towards their rooms. They usually left him until last given that he only relied on his stick. He waited until the only other person left behind in the room was a woman who never spoke. The poor creature spent her days staring into space. She had no idea where she was. Privately, Mansell had nicknamed her The Dowager of Doom. He thought of her as a signpost. An indication of what was to come for the rest of them. She was like a member of the advance party, one of the forward troops. Her body was still there but her spirit had already gone over the top. She wouldn't notice a thing.

He walked up to the cage and leant his stick against the wall. The culprit was squawking away. Mansell reached into his pocket and took out the loaded handkerchief. The four spongy balls were nestled in the centre. He paused for a moment wondering whether he should put all four in the cage at once or perhaps keep something back as a second line of attack. He was pondering the balls when suddenly he heard a voice from behind him.

'I've been keeping my eye on you, Mr Thomas.' Mansell nearly jumped out of his skin, thinking that the Head Jailer had returned unexpectedly. But the only person in the room was her, The Dowager of Doom.

'I saw what you did today with that block,' she said. 'Very Machiavellian.'

'I have no idea what you're on about,' he replied, which was partly true. He could feel his heart rate speeding up. But as he rolled one of the balls between his fingers he wondered what was the worst thing they could do to him? Arrest him? Send him to jail? Community service? Surely he was too old to gather rubbish from verges? He couldn't imagine the judge pronouncing the verdict – twenty-five years hard labour in Swansea jail for heartless avicide.

'Don't you think there's a better solution?' said the woman. Mansell was trying to think of a clever reply when she raised one arm and drew out a small key from the cuff of her cardigan.

'They think I'm totally doolally,' she said. 'And if you don't mind, I'd like to keep it that way. No one's going to chuck a ball at me like I'm some kind of dog. My legs don't work properly, that's true, but as far as I'm aware it hasn't affected my mental capacities.'

There was certainly nothing wrong with her eyesight, thought Mansell, as she fixed him a glacial stare.

'You won't be letting on either, *will* you now?' It wasn't really a question. She gestured for him to take the key. Mansell looked down at the spongy balls. Part of him had been looking forward to tomorrow morning's commotion, he realised.

'I think the budgie deserves to be liberated,' she whispered. But before she could add anything else they heard one of the staff marching down the corridor. Mansell stepped forward quickly and grabbed the key.

'Now then, Mrs Parry, you're next.'

The Dowager didn't even roll her eyes.

When they'd gone he returned to the cage. In one hand he held the key and in the other, a spongy ball. This must be the way God feels, thought Mansell. Will it be the key or the spongy ball for you? He slipped the key inside the lock. Part of him hoped it wouldn't fit, but it did. He turned it carefully and the bar slid back. The door swung open, just a little.

The bird was sitting on the top perch with its head turned looking suspiciously at the gap. Mansell opened the cage door fully and stood back. Nothing happened. He thinks it's a trap, he thought. 'Go on, you daft bugger.'

'Come on, Mr Thomas,' came a voice from the end of the corridor. 'Time for our beddy-byes!'

The bird cocked its head.

Mansell raised his walking stick in the air and nudged the cage until it shook. The budgie flew off its perch and landed on the threshold.

'Oh, for goodness sake, hurry up!' Mansell prodded the cage viciously, poking the wire with the stick.

'Mr Thomas?' The Head Jailer was approaching.

All of a sudden, the bird took flight. It landed briefly on top of the television then disappeared through the French doors. Mansell walked to the window. He could see the budgie on the branch of a cherry blossom. It looked completely out of place, glowing yellow against the sugar pink. Then it shrieked and flew off over the day-room roof. Mansell imagined it flying towards the sunset over fields of golden corn, stopping here and there on various trees, making its way on the summer breeze towards the sea. Of course, it would probably die of exhaustion within half a mile, he thought, given that it had not flown further than eighteen inches in the past however many years.

'Mr Thomas!' Very close now. Mansell shut the cage door and was about to do the same to the patio doors when, inspired by his undercover activities, he wondered whether he could make a run for it too? Hijack the neighbour's Massey Ferguson 35X as a getaway vehicle and speed on down to Narberth at a top speed of twenty-five miles an hour? But that would mean missing out on the fun the following morning. And what about the key? He couldn't be apprehended in possession of any incriminating evidence. The Dowager wouldn't be needing it now. His eyes scoured the room and came to rest on the fish tank with its solitary inhabitant. In the bottom left-hand corner there was a gaudy pirate's chest overflowing with long-lost plastic treasure.

Without hesitating, Mansell crossed the room and dropped the key into the tank. It landed perfectly on top of the treasure display, glinting as if it had always lived there.

'Mr Thomas!'

He grabbed his walking stick then remembered the poisoned balls. Now that the deed was done, he wouldn't be needing them either. He watched the fish swimming around. The water had a green tinge and there was a lot of slimy weed floating about in it. The fish came right up to the side and looked at Mansell as if it was trying to say something. Then after a moment it swam upwards, a little lopsidedly until it came to the surface. Mansell could see its mouth opening and closing, making ripples and little popping noises.

'So you want to make a racket too, do you?' Mansell's eyes narrowed. 'It's unnatural, floating around in your own waste. You should be in the sea, chasing prey. Someone should put you out of your misery.' Mansell felt for the sponge balls in the bottom of his pocket. He would have to dispose of them somehow. This was as good a place as any. He lifted the hanky out of his pocket and was about to tip the contents into the tank when the goldfish turned to gaze at him with enormous pleading eyes. Mansell thought of the liberated budgie making its way over golden cornfields.

'Oh, damn it all.'

'Oh, Mr Thomas!' Very close now.

Mansell grabbed an empty plastic vase from the sideboard, dunked it into the tank, scooped up the fish and made a dash for it outside where he lifted the grating off the storm drain with the end of his walking stick, poured the gloopy contents, complete with flapping orange fish, down into it, shoved the grating back into place with his boot and gave the vase a good fling into the nearest hydrangea.

'There you are, Mr Thomas! I was starting to think you'd done a runner.'

'I wish!' He shoved the loaded hanky back into his pocket and followed the giggling guard through the lounge and down the corridor towards his room.

You might be laughing now, he thought, but you wait. He could see it all, tomorrow's commotion, the general excitement, the escaped budgie, free at last, the fish released from slimy captivity. This was just the beginning.

You think I'm taking all this lying down?

You've got another thing coming.

BEING BOB

The Oscar-winning, BAFTA-nominated international screen actor, Hayden de Merle sprinted straight through the foyer of the BBC's Broadcasting House, and out into the morning sunshine of London's Portland Street, leaving a trail of open-mouthed security guards ('Sir! Your name tag if you please!'), a harassed receptionist ('I don't care who he is, get that TAG!'), and an adoring window cleaner ('Loved your last film!' 'Cheers mate! Here's a tag! It's signed!'). Hayden knew exactly where his car would be waiting. The space had been reserved with orange bollards just outside some foreign embassy draped with flags. He yanked open the driver's door.

'Bob, would you mind getting out?' Hayden was trying his best to sound calm. Any minute now, his publicist would be sprinting across the courtyard, hot on his heels, so there wasn't much time.

Bob was a good-natured kind of guy and happily clambered out.

'Problem, sir?'

'Not any more. Where's the central locking on this thing?'

Sure enough, in the distance, Hayden could hear the sound of expensive leather soles belting towards them.

'Here, sir.' Bob pointed to a button inside the door.

'And the windows?'

Bob pointed to some other controls.

Hayden jumped in and locked the doors. 'Thank you.' Bob was starting to look worried. 'Don't be alarmed!' Hayden raised his voice so he could be heard through the window. 'I'll look after it!' He started up the engine.

Matthew Thorneycroft's finely trimmed beard suddenly appeared in minute detail pressed up against the driver's window. 'What the hell are you doing?'

'I'm going for a drive.' Hayden smiled and reached up to adjust the rear-view mirror.

'But the programme's about to start!'

'I know.' Hayden pressed the button for the electric window so that it moved down a couple of inches. 'Bob? Would you mind moving that traffic cone, please?' Bob moved towards the cone.

'No! Don't you dare touch it!' screamed Matt. 'You can't just drive off! You've agreed to appear on the programme! We've been working on this for months!'

The 'this' that Matthew was referring to was Hayden's carefully managed withdrawal from the thespian world. Hayden ignored Matt and smiled at Bob.

'The bollard, there's a good chap.'

'Hayden, what's got in to you? They're going to be seriously pissed off. This could be really bad for you. We need to curate the next few months really carefully.'

That word again.

'Matt, could you please use language I understand? Curate? Isn't that what you do to things in a museum?'

'Open the bloody door!'

Hayden turned his attention to the dashboard and tried to figure out how to set the satnav. He pressed something on the display and a series of random maps appeared. 'Please make a U-turn. Please make a U-turn,' said the woman in a slightly bossy accent. 'Oh, keep your pants on,' muttered Hayden. He gave up on the satnav and turned his attention towards the buttons on the door, adjusting the height and angle of the wing mirrors. He was vaguely aware of a heated discussion outside the car regarding the orange traffic cone. Now Matthew was at the window, clinging to the top of it, with his fingers extending like some hungry squid into the space next to Hayden's forehead.

'Hayden, mate. Come back in. Do the programme. We'll talk about whatever it is that's bothering you once it's done. We can make whatever changes you like. I promise.'

Matthew had obviously come to some agreement with the driver regarding the traffic cone because Bob was now standing right in front of the car, hugging it with both arms.

'*We* are not going to make any changes, Matthew. *I'm* not your mate. And Bob, please move out of the way.' Hayden pressed what he thought was the button to close the window, started up the engine then put the automatic gear into 'D' for 'Drive'. The car immediately let out a long and whingeing *beep*.

'Now what?' Hayden muttered. Just as he realised that the beeping was probably due to the Park Assist, there was an even louder scream from outside the door. Matthew's hand had been caught in the closing window.

Beep.

'Matthew. Sorry, mate. That wasn't deliberate.'

Beep. Beep.

The Park Assist was really getting to him and all he could think of was moving away so that the bloody thing would stop. Bob stepped back from the front of the car and the reversing Park Assist beeps were now replaced by a different set, a semitone higher.

Beep! Beep!

There was a satisfying crunching noise as the car moved away.

That'll be the other bollard, thought Hayden as he pulled away. He caught a final glimpse of Bob hugging the traffic cone and Matthew jumping up and down, with rage or pain.

'What the ...!'

Beep.

'Come back!'

Beep.

'What am I going to...'

Beep. Beep.

Hayden pressed a load of random switches. 'Shut up!'

'Please make a U-turn,' said the satnav.

Hayden emerged on to Regent Street, making a right turn away from Oxford Circus. He was already halfway across when he realised he probably wasn't allowed to make the turn across four lanes of traffic.

'Idiot!' shouted a cyclist, swerving dramatically but somehow retaining enough balance to make a lewd gesture.

'Please make a U-turn,' said the satnav.

'Hayden! You've got to come back! Now!'

Somehow or other, Hayden's phone had connected to the car's loudspeaker, so when it rang, and Hayden was still prodding random buttons to switch off the irritating satnav, he inadvertently answered Matthew's call.

'Did I answer your call?'

There was a long pause.

'How should I know? You're talking to me, so you must have! Hayden, come back so that we can sort this out. Please. I'll send a car to pick you up.'

'From where?'

'The hotel.'

'I'm not going to the hotel.'

'Where are you going?'

'I'm not sure. Somewhere. Not here.'

Hayden reached for the dashboard. There must be a way of cutting off the call. His mobile had slipped under the passenger seat. He prodded more buttons, trying not to take his eyes off the road. He was in a lot of traffic and to his right he could see queues of people lining up to go into Madame Tussauds. He remembered Matthew's ideas about curating.

'Matt, is my puppet still in Madame Tussauds?'

'What?'

'You know, that sinister wax effigy?'

There was another long pause. Hayden was pretty sure he could hear Matt swigging something stiff, probably a whisky in hospitality.

'Please make a U-turn.'

'Christ. I'm in four lanes of traffic, how can I make a U-turn!'

'Who's in the car, Hayden?'

Hayden laughed.

'Seriously. Who's in the car? I thought we had an agreement that if you were going to have relationships, we needed to know. Is that what this is all about? You're really out of order. This wasn't the understanding. You need to look at your contract again if you think that... '

Miraculously, Hayden's next jab at the dashboard cut Matthew off in mid-sentence.

'Hurrah!' He jammed his foot on the brake just in time. He had been about to plough into the vehicle in front, a large and menacing-looking 4×4 which was painted in the deepest, darkest matt black paint. It seemed to be sucking all available daylight into itself. It's a mobile black hole, he thought. That's what I've disappeared into – a supermassive mobile black hole jam-packed with publicists and make-up artists and power-crazed agents.

Hayden took every turning or slip road that looked as if it might take him far away from London. At one stage, signposts offered him the choice between West and Midlands. Midlands sounded bad. He didn't want to be anywhere that was 'mid'. He wanted to be on the edge. In fact, so near the edge of things that he might fall off without anyone noticing. He had a vague recollection from filming some years earlier that the West could be reached along something called the M4. West was good. West eventually meant the edge. The furthest part of an entire country before the sea began. The last thing before Ireland.

'I bet you're really sulking now, aren't you?' said Hayden, addressing the satnav. 'What do you do with yourself when people aren't listening to you?'

'Please take the next exit on the left, then immediately turn left.'

Hayden put his foot down and sailed past the exit.

'Ha!'

The phone rang.

'Hayden!'

It was Ryan, one of Hayden's oldest friends. Finely trimmed Matthew must have spoken to him.

'How are you doing, mate?' Pause. 'Matthew tells me you're going through a bit of a rough patch.'

'I think you'll find that it's Matthew who's going through a rough patch. I've never felt better.'

'C'mon, mate. You don't have to hide anything from me. Matt said it might be difficult to talk, so you don't have to explain. Oh, God. Are you on hands free? Sorry... whoever you are.'

'No problem!' Hayden laughed. 'She won't be *too* offended.'

'Two? You're breaking up a bit. Does Maggie know? I mean, I thought things were looking up? It's not going to help your cause, mate.'

Hayden had no time to respond because just then he noticed some blue flashing lights approaching at speed in his rear-view mirror.

'Jeez,' said Hayden, glancing down at the speedometer. It said 95. 'Not good.'

'Too right. She'll be really pissed off if she hears about this. Sorry, whoever you are – both of you. Matthew's only looking after you, Hayden. I know he's a bit of a megalomaniac, but he's got your best interests at heart. Really.'

Hayden wasn't listening to Ryan. In fact, if it wasn't for the fact that he was trying to bring his speed down to an acceptable level without actually looking as if he was braking, he would be prodding the dashboard again, trying to cut off his friend's call. The police car must have been doing over a 100 because he was gaining incredibly quickly.

Hayden groaned as the speeding car drew level.

'Look, mate, don't worry. It's nothing that can't be handled. Maggie's great. She's forgiven you before. Quite a few times, let's be honest. That time in the Jacuzzi, and then at the Waldorf... you've got to admit, that was quite a stunt! Sorry, whoever you are. I mean, it was before your time. I would imagine. At least, what I mean is, I don't know that for sure as I don't know who you are, but... '

Hayden glanced at the speedometer, seventy-five. But the police car had flown past and showed no signs of stopping.

'Please leave the motorway at the next exit.'

'Oh, be quiet!'

'What?'

'Not you. Her!'

'That sounded like Vanessa. Is Vanessa with you?'

'What?'

'Is that Vanessa?'

Hayden would have answered that he couldn't remember anyone by that name but the cars ahead of him suddenly coalesced into a sea of red lights. Everyone was coming to a standstill and he was still doing well over seventy.

'Bloody hell!' Hayden slammed on the brake.

'Look mate, there's no need to swear, I'm only trying to help. I had no idea about any of this before Matt rang.'

The car came to a shuddering, leap frogging halt with a few inches to spare.

'Your route has been recalculated due to current traffic messages.'

'Vanessa, is that you?'

Hayden punched each one of the buttons surrounding him on the dashboard, the gear column, the door.

'It's tough being at the top mate, but you know, all you need to do is come back and I'm sure all this can be... '

Finally, Hayden cut off the call. He sank back in his seat, pushed up his sunglasses, closed his eyes and waited for the traffic to clear.

For the last few months, Matthew Thorneycroft had been trying to orchestrate a graceful retirement for Hayden. Ironically, this seemed to involve even more press activity than usual. At first, it had seemed like a good idea. An end to unpacking cases, having thirty versions of the same pair of jeans because the right pair was always in the wrong country. How many pairs of shoes did he have, he wondered? He'd lost count. In fact, beyond the age of twenty-two, when things had really hit the big time, he'd started to lose count of most things. He frequently woke unable to work out where he was. Yet, there was an underlying issue which neither he nor Matthew was prepared to address.

Most people dreamed of a life away from work. They had visions of finally growing into their skins. Being allowed to do what they liked as the person they really wanted to be. Free from bosses and HR departments, despotic line managers. Hayden, on the other hand, when he thought about retreating to his idyllic ranch in Idaho, found the prospect terrifying. He loved the horses and the hills, but he always went there as his last character, or the character he was about to become. He was Richard Nixon or a Viking warrior, a science genius or an undercover agent. He'd never actually been there when he was being himself.

His characters were amazing. They had incredible skills. But what was he, Hayden de Merle, good at? He was good at being other people. Escaping himself. Thinking about it, Hayden had probably only been himself for 25 per cent of his entire life.

On the move again, and keeping a close eye on the speedometer, he pondered the mechanics of Bob's accent and his East End drawl. How easy would it be to 'become' Bob? He tried to recall what his voice coach had told him about East End accents.

'You're awnly supposed to bleu the blady doors orf.'

Hayden was still 'being' Bob when the phone rang, so, unsurprisingly, he pressed exactly the right button to connect the call.

'Bob?' said a woman's voice.

'Yup,' answered Bob.

Hayden re-emerged and thought, *oh no*.

'Look,' she continued, 'I know you don't have much time because Hayden will soon be out of the studio so I'm just going to get straight to the point.'

Hayden made a sound, which was completely involuntary. The woman, whoever she was, took this as some indication that it was okay to carry on.

'I'm leaving you, Bob. I know it's a crap day to tell you. You've been looking forward to driving Hayden around but that's just it, isn't it? You always prefer to be at work. And why wouldn't you? I'd much prefer to be doing what you're doing than clearing out the cat-litter tray or wiping baby-sick off my shoulder. I had such a rubbish day yesterday. You've no idea. Trying to get the kids in the car for the school run, then sports day, then dentist appointments. And you got stressed within five minutes of being home, just because you couldn't find the telly remote! Get real Bob. We used to be such a team but since you got that swanky job, you're just not here anymore. Even when you are here, your head's somewhere else.'

Hayden made another noise. What was he to do? He couldn't come clean now, could he? Bob's wife had told him all these private things that Bob still had no knowledge of.

'Don't interrupt me, Bob,' she said. 'I've kept all this back for so long, I've just got to tell you as it is. I've packed the important stuff and there's a van coming later. We're going to the caravan in Wales. The kids will just think we're on holiday. I doubt they'll notice you're not there. Then we might go to my sister's. It's the best thing all round. I can get some proper help with the kids and you can look for your own bloody remote.'

This woman was clearly used to talking, thought Hayden. But it bothered him that she was used to Bob being so uncommunicative. Why was Bob just sitting there not saying anything? Was he just going to let her go? He concentrated on Bob's voice and said,

'I'm sorry.' There was a long silence on the other side. He was starting to wonder whether Bob's wife was still there. He thought he'd say something else just to find out.

'I've been a…' Hayden thought of all the derogatory words he'd heard Bob use for various other famous celebrities. 'Plonker.'

Another long silence, followed by something like a sob.

'You have no idea how long I've been waiting to hear those words.'

'I've been a plonker,' Hayden repeated, feeling rather proud of Bob.

'Not those words.'

Hayden thought back over what Bob had just said. 'I'm sorry?'

Another stifled sob. 'You have been a plonker, but it's so much easier to bear if you at least realise it. That's all I've ever wanted. For you to realise that you're being a plonker. Not all the time, obviously. Just sometimes. Well, quite often. I didn't marry a plonker. You weren't a plonker ten years ago.'

Hayden felt disappointed with Bob that he'd let things get this bad. What was the man thinking? Hayden didn't know what Bob's wife looked like. She could look like the back end of a bison for all he knew, but that was not the point. It wasn't all about looks. Hayden had received all kinds of offers since his own wife had left him. Some of the women had been jaw-droppingly stunning. But at the end of the day, what he really missed was a proper friend who didn't mind telling him when he was being a dipstick. Or a plonker. His own wife had been the most beautiful of them all as it turned out. Hayden had realised this too late, and now Bob was about to make the same mistake.

Bob's wife was still talking. She'd been listing Bob's misdemeanours. It was a long list.

'Well? Do you agree? Am I right to be upset?'

Hayden didn't want to damage Bob's improving reputation so he returned to the tried and tested formula.

'I've been a plonker. I'm sorry.'

'I know it's hard for you to talk.'

It really was hard for him to talk. Hayden was impressed with Bob's wife that she understood the circumstances.

'Do you really mean that?'

'Yup.'

'Do you want me to stay?'

Hayden was banking on the fact that Bob was a man of few words.

'Yup.'

Hayden glanced at himself in the rear-view mirror. He was even starting to pick up Bob's mannerisms.

'This doesn't mean that everything is all done and dusted, you know, that I'm going to put up with any old crap. We're both going to make an effort. Okay? We'll go on some date nights or something to remind us of why we're together. You're going to put your phone away and have a proper conversation with your kids. And you're going to stop being a plonker.'

'Yup.' Another pause.

'You know. You're even starting to sound like Hayden.'

Was his cover blown? He glanced at the rear-view mirror again and tried to imagine how Bob would respond. He needn't have worried. Bob's wife added, 'That's okay. He's a nice man.'

Hayden felt confused for Bob. For a moment, he felt

jealous that Bob's wife might have a bit of a thing for Hayden.

'He's a plonker,' said Hayden, reminding himself that he was pretending to be Bob.

'You don't mean that. You've always said he's a great bloke. You like him!'

Hayden felt proud of Hayden. Clearly, despite his fame, he still retained the common touch. He was, despite the publicists, the make-up artists, the carefully curated retirements, still a good egg.

'Look, I know you've got to go. We can talk about this later. I'm glad we sorted it all out. I'll cancel the van. Maybe we can go to the caravan on the weekend? Spend some proper time with the kids. Build sandcastles. Make a campfire. Maybe have a look at your schedule, will you? Bob? I love you.'

There was only one possible response. Hayden knew that Bob really had to nail this. It was the equivalent of the final curtain. Rapturous applause would only be possible if Bob put his heart and soul into the closing lines. Hayden concentrated on the shape of Bob's head, the curve of his mouth, how the sounds of the words would come out of those East End lips. He cleared his throat, and aimed for a tone a tad lower than the usual Bob. This was a man who was struggling with his own ineptitude after all. Searching for the right way forward.

'I love you too.'

Was it a clincher? Was it the tiny pause before the long bravo? He needed it to be unequivocal. He added the resounding, 'precious'.

'Oh, Bob! You haven't called me that for years. I love you, so much. Look, don't worry about anything here. And we never need to talk about this again. Ever. Now that I know how you really feel. I can't wait to see you later.'

Bob's wife hung up. Hayden felt elated in a way that he hadn't for years. It had been one of his best performances.

'What the hell have you done?' screamed Hayden at

Hayden.

'I've just saved a marriage, mate, that's what!'

'What if Bob's wife brings the whole thing up this evening and he has no idea what she's on about? What if he didn't want her to stay!'

'You heard her. She's not going to talk about it ever again. End of story. Happy days. She loves him. Bob's a lucky man.'

Hayden seemed content with Hayden's assessment of the situation. It was all very quiet in the car for the next hour and a half until the M4 ran out. Then Mrs Satnav woke up and started directing him through all sorts of bizarre junctions, leading to places names with unfeasibly large numbers of vowels in them.

He just about made it to the coast before the petrol gauge flashed red. He had no idea where he was. There was a beautiful estuary and a sea, which looked as if it stretched all the way to another continent. There were seagulls and even though the day had been uniformly grey, over the horizon the sun was setting in a clearing sky. This must be the edge I've been looking for, he thought. He watched as the last rays lit up the approaching good weather.

He went around the car and opened the passenger door. Reaching under the seat, he located his phone. He had 3 per cent battery life left. He'd obviously missed a few calls from Matthew Thorneycroft while Bob's wife had been on the phone. He probably owed him a call, even though he was a megalomaniac.

'Matt. It's Hayden.' Matthew let out a huge sigh and Hayden could tell that he was about to launch into a long report of what had happened since they'd last spoken. 'Look. No time to chat. My phone's about to die, so I'll be quick. I've had a rethink. Forget retirement. Curate a new scenario. I'm going to make another film. About an actor who saves a man's marriage during a long car journey. I'll act, direct, produce. What the hell, I might even fund it. It's going to be brilliant. I'm going to spend the rest of the month on the coast, fleshing out the script.'

Matthew Thorneycroft must have been hyperventilating. Hayden couldn't make head or tail of the noise at the other end.

'Trust me, Matt. The best is yet to come!'

'Where the fuck are you?'

Hayden held the phone away from his ear and studied the sunset. 'I have absolutely no idea. But it's beautiful, and very illuminating.'

On the other end of the line, there was a long squeak, like someone having his vital parts squeezed by a descending concrete block.

'Gotta dash!'

Whatever was about to come out of the phone was cut short.

A small fishing boat was chugging its way upriver after a day at sea. Hayden felt as if he'd arrived home too, even though he was lost and pretty much out of fuel. He looked down at the phone. One per cent left.

'I wonder if it would be a good idea?' asked Hayden.

'You aint got nothing to lose,' Bob replied.

Hayden scrolled through the numbers on his phone and stopped at his estranged wife's number.

'It worked for me,' added Bob.

Hayden didn't reply.

He was already dialling.

THE SIGNIFICANCE OF SWANS

In hindsight, it was the swans that gave 'them' away. Before then, I had never thought of swans as anything other than beautiful birds that graced an occasional river. They would glide by, imperious, mostly indifferent. They seemed oblivious, sleekly unconcerned.

But that day, when we saw seven of them flying over, I turned to my brother and said, 'Geese?'

'No,' he answered. He sounded sure, but there was a hint of bafflement in the voice. 'Swans.'

I stared closer. Yes, swans. 'I don't think I've ever seen one fly,' I said.

'Or calling,' he replied. 'Listen to that noise.'

What was it? A wail? A lullaby? It was both haunting and discordant.

I vaguely remembered a story that they only cried when they were about to die. Was that true? Or had I imagined it? I could have asked, but their song, if you could call it that, had us both transfixed.

We watched them as they flew past in formation. The pale-bluish January sky behind them was unusually free of clouds. We listened to their wails as they disappeared across the estuary. Shortly after that, we said our goodbyes, my brother and I.

I drove a hundred and sixty-six miles away from the sea.

The 'removals' began the following day, so we realised later. At first, they seemed like strange coincidences. In the county of Carmarthenshire alone, ten people had disappeared during the night. And when I say disappeared, I mean exactly that. They had left in such a way that the dents of their elbows were still there on soft cushions, their slumbering bodies still imprinted on mattress-toppers. 'You'll switch everything off, won't you, dear?', one wife had asked her husband. She had woken at 3am to find the lights still on and some noisy foreign film with subtitles and car crashes lighting up the living room. The doors were shut and the keys still inside. The windows were curtained and closed. The 'remote' was on the sofa arm. But Reg was gone. And so was Philipa from Reigate and Derek from Frome and Emma Barton from Moreton-in-Marsh.

The initial media reaction was uncharacteristically cautious. There was some logical explanation. An armed gang. Fraudulent tax evasion. Organised mass hysteria by a hitherto undiscovered religious sect. More information came to light. Overnight, twenty-one in Cambridge, ten in Norwich, fourteen in central London. And then, as the rest of the world began to wake up, so too in Boston, Kansas City and San Jose. This wasn't a UK phenomenon.

In one 24-hour period, 34,000 people, or thereabouts, had disappeared from the face of the earth. The television schedules were rearranged to accommodate longer current affairs programmes. That evening's newsreader was more solemn than usual. Small scraps of paper kept being handed to her by unidentified hands. A helpline for worried relatives was launched.

The following day, the same thing happened. The police were inundated. A&E departments were being mobbed by worried relatives convinced that their loved ones must have wandered out in a trance and somehow found themselves on the emergency wards. Even sensible people started talking about supernatural events. It was too odd to be a 'normal' occurrence. There must be something behind it. People, it was decided, were not just disappearing. They were being 'removed'. Some thing, some power or force that no one understood was taking them away. The experts on that evening's programme debated. It's a dormant cult that's come out into the open. People have cleverly covered their tracks. Ridiculous, others argued. Far too co-ordinated. Rays from outer space. 'They' are vaporising people in their beds. The audience laughed, a little too hysterically I thought. Someone said, sensibly, 'But there's no ash! There are no telltale remains.'

We had news of an immediate survey. Everyone, under penalty of something nasty but unspecified, was expected to complete an online questionnaire. The authorities needed to detect a pattern. Social media filled up with video clips. Look here! This is where she was! You can almost see the dent of her hand on the cushion! We put flour on the carpet... (surely not?) and there's no trail! No footprint! Aliens, someone said. Ridiculous! We imagined teeth and twirly tentacles. Don't be silly, someone else replied. Aliens aren't invisible. They leave trails of goo.

Each morning, there would be the daily updates. Morning television started running out of red pins with which to mark victims' locations. Then, one morning, there was a gloomy announcement. 'We're sorry,' they said. 'Toby, who's been doing the map, was removed last night. We'll do our best to find another pin-sticker-onner.'

Until then, it was like any other disaster. Misfortunes always seemed to happen to someone else's aunty or cousin or colleague that you once shared an office with five years ago. Then, the woman who ran the bakers disappeared. Then, our neighbour's wife. All of a sudden, the 'removed' became known to us. They became familiar. Every day there were more. We rang our children every morning. We messaged them constantly.

Things entered a new phase. It was decided that no one had disappeared from under anyone's nose. People ganged together. They formed sleep clubs. They would take it in turns to stay vigilant. No one would be removed under their watch. That was the theory. But all it took was a sleepy blink of an eye, or a sideways glance. Another one was gone. Families of the 'removed' tried to take 'sleep guardians' to court. They'd been negligent in their duties of care. People chanted on courtroom steps. They held placards. 'That's all very well,' said the courtroom liaison officer in a blaze of flashlights, 'but the judge was removed last night. Case is adjourned.' The sleep clubs were disbanded.

The questionnaires flooded back and were analysed. The rich, the poor, the important, the weak, the strong – no one was safe. Whatever was doing the 'removing' was no respecter of colour or politics or bank statements. The poorer counties claimed that they were suffering greater numbers of removals. The figures disagreed.

Things began to get hysterical. Everywhere, people seemed to be shouting and screaming at everyone else. People who had got used to blaming someone else for all the things that went wrong in their lives were beside themselves. Someone was definitely to blame. And when they found out who they were, there would be hell to pay. They would be lined up against a wall and be made to suffer horribly for inflicting such pain on them, personally. How dare they?

Then, suddenly, it was like a long chain which had been stretched too far. The links that had held fast for so long just popped. The joints opened up and the whole thing sprang apart. The people that had held our world together – the last baker, the last bus driver, the last postman – all of a sudden, they were gone. It didn't matter if you were rich or famous, influential and had thousands of friends on Facebook, what mattered was whether you knew how to fix a generator, or get the car started. It only slowly occurred to us that even if you could get the car started, soon there would be no petrol. And even if there was petrol, from some far-flung depot, the man who drove the lorry would soon be gone.

We rang our children and pleaded with them to come 'home'. But it was already too late. The trains weren't running.

No matter, we said, we'll walk. 'Mum, when was the last time you walked a hundred and eight miles? There are looters! Maybe murderers!' They were right. At least, there were looters. To start with. Then even the looters realised that no one with half a brain wanted Rolex watches any more. What we wanted was someone who had flour and who remembered how to bake a loaf. We rang our children and said, 'This might be the last time. We hear the electricity is going.' 'We'll be alright,' they said. 'Will you and Dad be okay?' 'It will stop soon,' we replied. The following day, the power was down, so there was no more landline. We managed one last call to the oil suppliers' answerphone before the mobile phone gave up.

'We should have charged it overnight,' I said feebly.

'It was going to go eventually,' you said.

'But we could have said goodbye to the kids,' I cried, or rather, wailed.

'You said goodbye yesterday. And the day before.' It occurred to me that I had married a really heartless man. You were in shock. I realise that now.

'How will we know if they're okay?' I wailed some more.

'You're not going to know,' you said. 'You'd better get used to it. We're not going to know anything any more. We just have to go from day to day. It's all we have. Maybe they're already gone.'

'Who?'

'The kids.'

I was speechless.

The world became surprisingly quiet. The last few cars owned by people who'd stockpiled fuel stopped running. There were no pilots, no planes. The air traffic control had lost all their trained staff. There were no policemen and surprisingly little crime. We'd been given some seed potatoes by the farmer next door before he disappeared. We planted them by hand because his tractor had run out of diesel. Amazingly, they grew, so that winter wasn't too bad. I'd been reading my cookbooks for using our glut of gooseberries. I made tons of jam. But then, although the gooseberries kept on coming, I ran out of sugar. I came across a recipe for fondant mushrooms with glacé cherry mousse and a white wine jus. I laughed so much I gave myself an asthma attack. I laughed some more. Then I started to cry.

'I can't eat gooseberries without sugar,' you said. You'd always loved your food. I'm sure that was the point at which you gave up. I don't think THEY could have realised it, but it was pretty good timing from your point of view.

When I woke the next day I could have sworn I heard you sigh with relief. Another morning, successfully arrived at, I thought.

'Cup of incredibly weak tea?' I joked in the November half-light. But you didn't answer. I turned to face you and the duvet was still warm and shaped around you, but hollowed out.

'Graham?' I said, but I knew you weren't there. I sat for a long while by your side of the bed, stroking the shape of the bedding gently, willing it to stay in your shape.

I couldn't sleep in our bed after that. I couldn't bear the thought of disturbing your shape, the void in the duvet. Over time the shape caved in. The months dragged on. Out on the side of our hill, seven miles from town, there was no sign of anyone any more. No cars had passed for over a year. I tried the electricity from time to time, in the vain hope that something had happened, that civilisation had somehow got back on its feet. But there was nothing.

I planted potatoes. I harvested potatoes. I walked as far as I dared in a day to gather anything that grew, anything I could propagate. I learned to cook on the log burner or ate things raw. I grew peas and worked my way through the stockpile of gooseberry jam. One evening, for supper, I had half a baked potato with boiled peas in a gooseberry jam jus. I used the pages from the fancy cookbooks to keep the fires going. The two most important things were keeping warm and eating. The hedges grew tall and unkempt which was a good thing, I realised. For parts of the year they were full of blackberries, rosehips and sloes. Without pesticides, the mushrooms came back to the fields. A mushroom cooked in wood ash is surprisingly tasty.

I took a perverse pleasure in seeing my neighbour's garden fill up with tasty baby nettles and docks. A space that had seemed under daily attack from power tools and chemicals breathed a sigh of relief, filled out and came back to life. The butterflies, the bees, the fox returned. What had been a sterile lawn was now pockmarked with a wonderful array of molehills. Some mornings, I'd go out there just to count the new mounds. It wasn't all bad.

On my long walks, looking for firewood and food, I would think of the kids, I would think of my brother. Now and again when it all got too much, I'd sit on your side of the bed and talk to what was left of your shape in the duvet. I hoped that wherever you were it wasn't too painful.

Four years had gone by and there had been no signs of life. One day, I ventured to the nearest town. Weeds were growing on the main street. The drainpipes had filled with leaves and some had collapsed. A few shop fronts had been boarded up but in other ways it seemed surprisingly untouched. People had gone quickly, it seemed, before there was too much chaos. The dogs must have gone too, I realised. I had imagined dangerous bloodthirsty packs. Perhaps they'd all been put down as an act of kindness? Perhaps THEY liked dogs? I looked for what I could but there was nothing left. Hardly a match.

I was convinced that I would have been noticed that day. I was fully prepared not to wake up the following morning, or find myself in some strange place full of weird sounds and blue flashing lights. But I woke in the spare bed as usual and when I opened my eyes, I realised with clarity and some degree of dismay, that that was it. Whatever had removed everyone else did not intend to come back for me. I felt strangely betrayed.

Things were getting very bare. In my tiredness, I had let the fire go out. I scoured the house for paper to help me light it. I was down to my last match. I couldn't afford to let it go out again. I had whittled my books down to the essential few, poetry, vegetable gardening and DIY. All the others had gone on the fire. I emptied a drawer and realised to my joy that I had lined it with a copy of the *Guardian* from years before. I looked at the date. A week after the first removals. There were long discussions on various theories, and then the results of the first questionnaire analysis. I took out the newspaper and scrunched it into a ball. At the door to the log burner, I hesitated. Perhaps this was the last written record? In generations to come, when none of the technology could be made to work, this might be the last piece of evidence. The story of the demise of the human race was about to disappear into my fire. But I had to keep warm.

Very carefully, I lit the last match. I held it to the edge of a page. The word 'swan' glared out at me from the crumpled mass. I poked the ball with a twig. 'I saw swans,' said the sentence. I put my hands in the burner to disentangle the page. I tried to flatten it without stopping the flames. 'Man sees seven swans,' said the headline, and my hands went cold. 'Mr Hopkins from Stirling insists that this is of some importance, given recent events. However, the Prime Minister, interviewed on Radio 4, says that there are no resources to pursue this line of enquiry.' There was more to the interview, but the flame curled around the paper. I poked again and the flame stuttered. I stood back, fearing that I would make the fire go out. I placed thin twigs and wiry branches around the sheet then peered again. 'Believe me,' says Mr Hopkins, 'this has some significance. The point is, you're all asking the wrong questions.' The paper erupted in flames and the twigs crackled. The report was gone. I should have been glad that the fire had taken hold, but all I could think of was that I had destroyed the one clue that might have made a difference. Had the swans really been that important? Was that why I was still here? In which case, was my brother still by the sea, living like me, stockpiling wood and surviving off potatoes and some variety of jam? Was Mr Hopkins still in Stirling?

The evening closed in. I fed the fire its rations. I thought about my children and found myself hoping that they might have noticed the birds. It was unlikely. They hardly looked up from their devices. I blamed myself for their irrelevant, competitive education. I asked myself seriously when was the last time I had walked a hundred and sixty-six miles to the coast. But if, by some miracle, my children had noticed something, they might walk all the way here only to find me gone. What then? I sat by your side of the bed and plumped up the duvet in an attempt to create your shape. I asked you so many questions but didn't get any answers.

That evening I baked a small potato in the burner. I imagined cheese and butter then wondered, what had happened to all the cows? By the light of the fire, I fixed the holes in my socks and sewed patches on my jeans. I needed to get ready for some kind of journey, I was sure of that. But which one? I'd make my decision in the morning, I decided. After a good night's sleep.

OH, HANAMI
(or Fall Seven Times and Stand Up Eight)

Interviewer:	*So, for the sake of our viewers, would you be so kind as to explain what is meant by 'Hanami'?*
Japanese gardener:	*The word 'Hanami' comes from 'hana' which means flower, and 'mi' which means to view. So: 'flower viewing' — first mentioned by the novelist, Murasaki Shikibu in* The Tale of Genji. *The cherry blossoms, the sakura, remind us of the transience of life. The cherry trees only blossom for two or three weeks. They are beautiful, dazzling, bright and fleeting, just like us.*

The interviewer and the elderly Japanese gardener turned to admire the landscape in the background. The camera panned out, over the gardener's head, to show the scene in detail. Hundreds of cherry blossom trees lined a gravel path, which meandered up a grassy slope. There were lavender-coloured hills in the distance, and above it all, a dazzling blue sky.

Jim clutched the top of his walking stick and leaned forward to scrutinise the intense colours and incredible definition on the brand new UHD television screen his son Danny had bought before Christmas. There was a pause in the interview; the kind of pause you would have if you'd walked to the top of a ridge and, all of a sudden, an entire glorious valley was laid out before you, and you couldn't catch your breath quickly enough to find the words to describe it.

The interviewer held back the next question, anticipating the viewers' need for a moment's contemplation. The gardener also waited, knowingly, it seemed, and his chest rose as he inhaled deeply. Then, as if the whole thing had been perfectly choreographed, the gardener exhaled, and a breeze, like an incoming wave, moved through the branches, ruffling the blossoms just enough for some of them to loosen and drift across the scene like a shimmer of spray.

> *Japanese gardener:* *You see! Even now, the petals come away.*
> *The time we waited for is already passing.*

The gardener said this to the interviewer, but he turned to look directly at the camera. At Jim.

A voice from the landing.

'Hey, Dad? Are you okay down there?'

Down there, in the sitting room, is what his son meant. But, as Jim stared at the cherry trees, he realised that 'down there' was exactly where he'd been. Down there, scrabbling to make a living; looking down at the planting, down at the harvest, down at the plough, the roller and the drill.

'Dad?'

'Yes, yes!' Jim replied. 'Still breathing!' To eliminate any doubt.

The Japanese gardener seemed to be waiting for Jim to pay attention. He looked like a man who would have an answer for all of life's knotty questions. How old was he? Fifty or ninety? Ageless. Serene. Rooted in his world, like one of his own trees. The elderly man raised his hand in an elegant gesture, inviting the camera to follow his gaze, through the dark branches, over the blossom, to the skies and the snow-covered mountains beyond.

'Plant some in the orchard, you mean?'

Jim knew Danny had heard him properly the first time, so he concentrated on the melting crust of demerara sugar on top of his porridge.

'No, I mean plant them in the barley field.' Which is what

I just said, Jim thought, but he didn't say this out loud.

Jim swallowed a mouthful of porridge but didn't look up. Danny was probably rolling his eyes, covertly, at Jim's daughter-in-law, Sue, which is what he usually did when he didn't like something.

'Where are we going to plant the *barley*?'

'Somewhere else.'

Danny stopped chewing his toast. There was a noisy swallow, then a well-controlled sigh.

'There *isn't* anywhere else. We're already renting three fields from next door.'

A voice from upstairs.

'MUM! I can't find my English file. Is it down there?'

Sue got up from the table and crossed the room to the settle, where she rummaged through a pile of newspapers and magazines.

'How many are you thinking?' asked Danny.

Jim considered his porridge and made a calculation.

'A hundred. Maybe a hundred and twenty.'

The butter knife fell off Danny's plate.

'At least to start with. We'll see how it goes.'

Another shout from upstairs.

'MUM! Don't worry! I've FOUND it!'

'Bloody hell.' Sue returned to the table. 'Every morning! I'll be glad when she's gone to Uni.'

'*If* she goes,' said Danny.

'She'll pass.'

'It's not that. I'm not sure we can afford the fees this time, if we're going to be one field short.'

Jim ignored the last spiky comment. It was one of those 'kick the door so the latch can hear' kind of comments that Danny often resorted to, not wanting all-out open warfare at the kitchen table.

After dropping Louise at school, Danny and Sue were heading off to the Three Counties Show, near Malvern.

Ordinarily, they would have had a last minute attempt at persuading Jim to go with them. But this morning, they packed the Land Rover with wellington boots and jackets and umbrellas and a whole load of paraphernalia without so much as a 'Ferguson-Thirty-Five'.

'Come on, Louise!' Danny hollered from the front door. He turned to Jim, who was still at the table.

'We'll have a little chat later.'

Jim raised his hand to show that he wasn't going deaf and thought, I won't be needing any little chats later.

There was a thunderous noise from the staircase and Louise came bursting into the room with her bag and coat flying. She shot straight out of the front door and slammed it so hard that all the jugs on the dresser rattled in disapproval. Jim polished off his porridge and counted one, two. Louise flew back in, clip-clopping across the flagstones in heels that were far too high and a skirt that was far too tight. He didn't look up but was enveloped in a rough hug that left him in a fog of perfume.

'See you later, Gramps! Be GOOD!'

The house shook for a second time and the Land Rover's engine started up. Jim listened to the vehicle roar up the farm lane, idle briefly as it met the main road, and speed off in the direction of Hereford.

> *Japanese gardener: Sakura petals fall before they've withered, like the Samurai who were destined to die young. Why do we neglect to revel in life when it can end at any moment? We are so often blessed, but fail to see it. The sakura remind us to pay attention.*

'A hundred and thirty-seven?'

It was suppertime and the conversation had turned towards Danny's little chat.

'I think that should do it,' added Jim, 'allowing for decent pathways in between.'

'Pathways? For what?'

'People. To walk around, and admire the blossoms. The sakura.'

'Jeez.' Danny plunged his knife and fork into one of the beef and onion pies they'd brought back from the show.

Jim turned to Sue. 'Very nice pie.'

'Thank you.' She wasn't taking sides.

'So. Are we selling cherries now?'

'No. They're purely ornamental.'

'Since when can we afford to plant things that are "purely ornamental"?'

Louise, who had been eating her food with a fork in one hand whilst checking her phone with the other, looked up.

'What's up, Gramps?'

Jim placed his cutlery down to rest either side of his plate. He thought of the gardener's long inhalation.

'I'm going to plant the barley field with cherry trees. Sakura – that's what they call them in Japan.'

'Awesome!'

'And when they're big enough, I'll open it up to the public so that we can celebrate *Hanami*.'

'What's that?'

'That's what they call the festival. People sit under the cherry trees and have picnics and celebrate life. Or rather, celebrate – how did they put it? – the fleeting nature of life. Here one minute and gone the next. Sometimes, the gardens are opened at night, with lanterns.'

'*Cool!* Can I bring my friends?'

'In Herefordshire! In April! Dad, what's got in to you? No one's going to want to wander around a soggy field of cherry trees in a British spring!'

'Gravel paths.'

'You don't even like the Japanese!'

'I never said that.'

'Your cousin came back from the war weighing five stone. How many times have you told us that story?'

It was true. Jim's uncle had been a Japanese prisoner of war. He'd come back a skeleton, stooping and emaciated.

'We did terrible things too.'

'You won't get planning permission. Change of land use.'

We'll see about that, thought Jim.

'When do you start planting, Gramps?'

'This autumn. But I need to order them first. I might drive down to the garden centre tomorrow to get some ideas.'

Jim looked up at Danny, thinking he might offer to drive him on the grounds that he was eighty-two and no one seemed keen for him to be in charge of anything meaningful. But Danny was concentrating on his pie. So was Sue. Louise was looking at her phone again. Her wavy auburn hair had been ironed flat and it hung like a curtain around her face. Jim hadn't noticed until now, but she was wearing a thick layer of make-up that made her look like something that had fallen out of an oil painting. And what were those things above her eyes? Two perfectly illustrated arcs that appeared to have been borrowed from someone else. Louise must have mistaken his own raised eyebrow for a request, because when she looked up at him, she jumped as if she'd just snapped out of a dream.

'No problem! I'll drive you!'

Saturday. The man at the garden centre was trying to be helpful but there were so many things to consider.

The size?

Big.

The available space?

Plenty.

The colour? Pink? White? There's even a variety of creamy yellow.

Weeping, column, standard, double or single flowers, pot or bare root, good autumn colour or interesting bark?

Jim tried to smile, but he could feel his left eye twitching.

'What do you think, Louise?'

Louise, who didn't appear to have been listening to any of it, dragged her eyes away from the screen just long enough to declare, 'Big, *normal* shaped trees. Definitely not *weeping*. We don't want anything sad. Pink *and* white; definitely *not* lemon. And it says here single flowers are best for bees, Gramps, but I guess you could have both types seeing as there'll be so many.'

'There you go, then – what my granddaughter says.' Louise raised her face briefly and gave them a dazzling smile framed by intense maroon lipstick. How she could read that thing and walk around without bumping into the topiary displays was beyond him.

How many did they require?

'A hundred and thirty-seven.'

The man gave a low whistle, swiped the pencil from above his ear and made some enthusiastic marks on his notepad.

'We can give you a discount, of course.'

'A rough quote?'

'Sure thing.'

'Wow. That's a lot.' They were back in the car and Louise was eyeing the total at the end of a long list. Jim held it up for her to see.

'Dad'll have a fit.'

'It's not his money.'

Louise pursed her lips, then after concentrating on the paper for the longest time he'd ever seen her take her eyes off her phone, added, 'We'll just have to search online. Get you a better deal.' She started up the engine.

'Pretend Porsche or pretend Aston Martin?'

Jim rubbed his chin.

'Pretend Lamborghini, I reckon.'

'Orange?'

'Of course.'

Jim had been walking the barley field, surveying the ground and planning the sakura path. They'd had some downpours that morning, so he was washing the clay off his wellingtons under the tap by the side of the house. Poking his foot under the jet of water, trying to get as much mud off without having to bend down, he heard voices, coming through the vent in the wall. That was the peculiar thing about the vent. Any conversation in the kitchen was amplified. People forgot that. You could hear every word.

'It's going to cost a fortune!'

'It's his farm.'

'Don't I know it! What am I supposed to do? Stand by and let him ruin an entire field? It could be dementia. This is how it starts, you know. Weird behaviour.'

'There's nothing wrong with him.'

'*Hanami!* What's that all about?'

'Louise says he saw a programme on telly.'

There was a long pause. Jim thought Danny was probably rolling his eyes.

Flossie, the dog, who'd followed Jim up from the field, loitered next to him, panting loudly. Jim brought his finger up to his lips.

'Shhh.' Flossie plonked her bottom on the concrete path and waited for Jim's next move.

'Who's going to plant them all? If he thinks I've got time to stick a hundred and thirty-seven trees in the ground, he's got another thing coming.'

'Louise says we could watch a recording.'

'What? And give him more encouragement? It's about time she went off to Uni. That's if we still have a farm to support us all by the time *he's* finished with it. Cherry blossoms! We're going to be a laughing stock!'

'That's what's bothering you.'

'No. It's the cost, isn't it?'

'I told you we shouldn't have bought that new telly.'

Jim was in Louise's bedroom staring at her computer screen as she searched for tree wholesalers.

'This one's got a good website.' The little arrow on the screen shot upwards and clicked on various symbols until Jim was presented with a catalogue of cherry trees.

'They're *much* cheaper than the garden centre!'

'No overheads.'

Louise scrolled through the list until it made his head spin.

'We could make a spreadsheet to compare costs.'

'Don't forget, delivery.'

A shout from downstairs.

'Louise! I hope you're getting on with your revision!'

Louise made a face and carried on scrolling. How pretty she was without the layers of spray paint, thought Jim.

'You're just like your grandmother, you know.'

'I miss Granny.' Jim knew she meant it, but for the time being, her real attention was elsewhere. Bits of text flew around the screen. Pictures flashed here and there. Diagrams collided with special offers and customer reviews. There were tables and charts.

Jim felt seasick.

'There!' Louise, hit the final key with a flourish, making the printer spring into life. A spreadsheet spluttered out of the machine.

Jim laughed when he saw the title: Oh, Hanami!

'Don't worry, Gramps, I'll defend you. Now *scoot* before I get into trouble!'

> *Japanese gardener:* *At first, Hanami was enjoyed only by wealthy members of the court. But the samurai, Toyotomi Hideyoshi, believed that by bringing Hanami to ordinary people, it would influence them in a positive way. He believed that all great warriors needed to be cultured.*

'Hello, Mr Barber. We haven't seen you here for a while.'

She was being polite. Jim was pretty sure he'd never stepped foot inside the town library. But Karen, the librarian, was a neighbour's daughter, so that was a good start given that he felt very out of place.

They exchanged pleasantries: the weather, how was the family at home, how he must miss his wife, the price of lamb.

'So, how can I help?'

'I'm looking for books on cherry trees.'

She raised an eyebrow but led the way to the relevant section.

'Do you have your driving licence?'

Jim wondered what on earth his ability to drive had to do with reading books.

'ID.'

Jim was even more alarmed.

'For the library card. In case you want to take something home.'

'Oh, yes. If I see one I like.'

'One!' She had a voice that reminded Jim of the owl that lived in the barn. 'Twelve, more like! Isn't that right, Audrey?'

A lady in the corner raised her head and smiled.

'Audrey is one of our regulars. When was the last time you had something for nothing, Mr Barber? That's why we love our libraries, isn't it Audrey?'

A queue was forming at the counter.

'I'm sure Audrey will help if you can't find what you're

looking for.'

Karen turned away, but just when it looked like she was going to leave him in peace to search through the gardening slash horticulture section on his own, she leaned in, alarmingly close and whispered, 'Widowed last year!'

Audrey flashed him a smile. She looked very pink in her pink blouse and slightly fluffy-looking pink cardigan. In fact, she made him think of a good-looking cherry tree. A very neat cherry tree that may once have been an English teacher. This last thought made him feel particularly nervous. He returned the smile, just to be polite, then turned to concentrate on the bookshelf.

Jim was still going through the books. Who would have thought there would be so many different varieties?

Amanogawa
Kanzan
Okame
Shirofugen
Yoshino
Tai-haku
Shirotae

Where would he start? There were more English sounding names too:

Snow Goose
Pandora
Blushing Bride.

The last made him think of the day he and Anne had got married. She would probably be a bit mystified by his plan, he thought, but she always came round in the end. He would order a *Blushing Bride*, he decided, and plant it in the corner of the barley field, where there was the best view of the Welsh hills in the distance, where they'd scattered her ashes eighteen months earlier.

But this was no time for dwelling. He needed to make a

list. He sat down at the table and dug his hand into his jacket pocket, pulling out the pencil he'd brought. He'd forgotten to bring his notebook, he realised, so he fumbled around in his pockets for a scrap of paper. He found one, a long shop receipt from the farmers' co-op. But when he tugged it out, it was tangled in a piece of orange baler twine. A random collection of coins, bits of straw and Werther's Original Creamy Toffees spilled on to the library floor.

'Damn.'

A coin of undetectable denomination rolled its way under the tables. Jim heard it ping, somewhere, against a table leg, and he looked up to see Audrey bending down to retrieve it. Her hips were better than his, he thought, and before he knew it, she'd made her way across the room with the shiny pound and a couple of twenty pence pieces she'd picked up along the way.

She placed them on the table in front of him and, seeing the books, said, 'Cherry blossoms! My favourite!' Then in an altogether different tone of voice, said, *Loveliest of trees, the cherry now.'* Audrey looked at him as if she'd just uttered a piece of secret code that he was supposed to understand. It reminded him of all those other times people had looked at him, expecting him to know the answers to everything. He could tell she was about to add something, possibly another test, so he said, out of panic more than anything else, 'I'm planting a cherry orchard!'

> *Japanese gardener:* There are over 600 cherry blossom cultivars in Japan. Amanogawa is very popular. It means, 'River of the sky'.
>
> *Interviewer:* That's beautiful.
>
> *Japanese gardener:* Another is Kanzan, which means, literally, 'bordering the mountain'. But translations don't convey everything, do they? For Japanese people, Kanzan

invokes the idea of a perfect mountain village, a mountain remembered from childhood, or one which is conjured in a poem, or a beautiful painting.

Jim had been marking out the field with a wooden mallet and little wooden stakes to show where the cherry trees should be. It was quite a task with a dodgy hip. He'd paced the distances between them, staggering the rows so that they wouldn't look regimental. He wanted a sea of blossom, visible from space, or at the very least, the top of the Black Mountains. He'd just hammered in the fifth post with a wooden mallet, thinking five down, only another hundred and thirty-two to go, when he heard a series of scraping noises coming from the road. There was an ear-piercing screech, a thud, then a man's voice, swearing. Jim grabbed the walking stick that was leaning on the fence and walked up to the corner of the hedge to see what had happened. There, in the middle of the road, was a cyclist, sprawled, face down, but evidently still alive. He seemed to be clad from head to toe in bright blue, skin-tight gear.

The man got up with a groan, dusted himself down and rubbed various parts of himself that would be covered in bruises as blue as his gear by the following morning. The bike was upside down and embedded in the hedge.

'You alright there?' asked Jim.

The man unhooked his alien-looking lozenge-shaped cycling helmet and turned towards him. He was a lad, rather than a man.

'Oh, yeah, thanks. Just about. Bloody pothole.'

He hobbled across the road to retrieve his bike and Jim walked out towards him. His knee was bleeding badly.

'Good job there isn't much traffic. You're a bit of a mess.' The blue fabric was shredded to bits and turning purple with blood.

'Come up to the house. We'll get you some bandage.'

The lad began wheeling the misshapen bike up the lane.

'I'm interrupting your work.' He'd noticed Jim's wooden mallet. 'Sorry.'

'No matter. I needed a rest. When I was young, like you, I suspect I could have done the whole field in the time it's taken me to do five. Old crock that I am.'

Anthony glanced across at Jim's work in progress.

'How about I trade you some help for a bandage and a cup of tea? I'm Anthony.'

They shook hands and Jim couldn't help admiring the lad's impressive physique, perfectly designed for a spot of stake walloping.

'Well, Anthony. That sounds like a bargain!'

> *Japanese gardener: This variety is called Shirotae, or the Mount Fuji tree, because the pale blossoms that clothe the dark branches are supposed to look like the snowdrifts caught in the ravines of Mount Fuji.*
>
> *This one, Tai-haku, or The Great White Cherry, was thought to have died out. But one was discovered in a remote Sussex garden, owned by a Mrs Freeman. It was reintroduced to Japan by Collingwood Ingram. The original name for this tree is Akatsuki, which means 'daybreak' or 'dawn' – for good reason. When in flower, it looks as if it is lit from within. So you see, every Tai-haku in the world is descended from Mrs Freeman's tree in Winchelsea.*

'He's gorgeous!' Louise was on the phone again, evidently

under the impression that she was hissing out of earshot while the rest of them were around the table having tea.

'Anthony was a dab hand with the stakes,' said Jim, trying to draw attention away from the conversation in the hallway. 'Despite his injury.'

Anthony raised his knee to table height to illustrate the generous layer of crepe bandage wrapped around his leg.

Louise came back in. On tiptoes, for some reason. Jim watched her as she sidled delicately along the bench, leaving a decent gap between her and the visitor. Her phone was out of sight.

'So where are you from, Anthony?' said Danny.

Jim could tell where this conversation was going so he answered on his behalf. 'Anthony is from Bristol, aren't you Anthony? He's studying to be a lawyer. He's been a great help.'

'No, *really* from? Where were you from, before Bristol?'

Louise stiffened up and shot her father a warning glare.

'My dad was born in Bath, and my grandfather was born in Newport. My great-grandfather was born in Bristol. So we haven't gone far. Around in circles.'

Louise smiled and picked up the plate of cake.

'Cider cake, Anthony?'

Anthony took a piece.

'What do you think of my father's crazy plan then?'

Jim wondered when it was that his son had turned into a human pine cone, all knobbly and rough-edged.

'Sounds great!' said Anthony. 'Very ambitious. Not many people have your father's vision. We need more trees.'

There was an uncomfortable pause where Danny would normally have rolled his eyes. Then Anthony added, right out of the blue and without having consulted Jim on the matter at all,

'I'll be back to help plant the actual trees. That is, when you're ready, Jim. Just let me know. I'll leave you my number.'

Anthony bit into his slice of cake and turned to Louise.

'Top cake.'

Jim was pretty sure he saw him wink at her.

Danny must have seen it too because there was a long, laborious intake of breath as he cleared his throat to say something truly acerbic but Sue intervened.

'Eat some cake, Danny.' And the plate of traditional Herefordshire Cider Cake was thrust under his nose before he could say 'Leyland Two-Seven-Two with synchromesh gears'.

> *Japanese gardener:*   *We have a word in Japanese, Kisetsukan, roughly translated it means 'to be aware of the cycle of the seasons'. Hanami is planned, anticipated and most importantly of all, involves everyone. Is there an equivalent in the West? A natural event, which brings the entire population together?*
>
> *Interviewer:*   *I'm not sure. Perhaps our viewers could let us know?*
>
> *Japanese gardener:*   *Hanami is the most popular, but we also have the viewing of autumn leaves – Momijigari, moon viewing – Tsukimi, and snow viewing – Yukimi. For every season, there is an excuse, if you like, for people to gather together with those that are important to them.*

The man leapt out of the lorry cabin and walked up to Jim, clipboard in hand. 'Mr Barber?'

'That's me.'

The man handed him a short plastic stick. Jim wasn't quite sure what he was supposed to do with the stick, until he was also handed some kind of electronic device and gestured for him to make a squiggle on the screen.

'No worries, it never looks like your writing. So, where do you want these one hundred and thirty-seven cherry trees?' He made it sound like a malediction. 'Orchard?'

'No. Field.'

'Planting an arboretum?'

It was bad enough explaining himself to his own family. 'You could say that.'

They unloaded the trees on to big tarpaulin sheets.

'Good luck!' said the driver once they'd finished, and the truck left in a cloud of amazement. Perhaps Danny was right? Perhaps he was losing his marbles? Jim checked over the trees. They didn't look very robust. It was difficult to imagine the stunning hillside of sakura they were meant to become. Would they even grow into anything worth looking at before he dropped dead? That was the question. Could he hurry them up with copious amounts of cow dung? But then, perhaps that wasn't the point? It was almost as if the old gardener was there at his shoulder, urging him on, despite all his doubts.

There was someone standing at his shoulder, as it happened. Danny.

'They gave me three for free because it was a big order!'

Danny just shook his head, taking in the significance of the miserable cherry trees and would probably have said something dispiriting, if it wasn't for what happened next; three cars, a minibus and a massive jeep with a flatbed trailer and a mini digger loaded on to it came roaring down the lane.

'Here come the troops!'

Louise was the first to jump out, closely followed by Anthony, then Louise's friends from Uni who were all on a reading week, and Anthony's friends from work, Audrey's son and teenage grandchildren, and finally, the librarian, Karen, along with two of her colleagues. And because Danny was still standing next to Jim, everyone was under the impression that he was also there to help. There was a lot of hand shaking.

'Do we know all these people?' asked Danny.

'No. But we soon will.'

Japanese gardener:	*So, here, along this ridge, I have planted young trees.*
Interviewer:	*They're lovely. How long have they been here?*
Japanese gardener:	*Nearly eight years. I planted them along the waterline.*
Interviewer:	*Waterline?*
Japanese gardener:	*Yes. Where we are standing now, this is how far the water came in 2011, at the time of the tsunami.*
Interviewer:	*Really? But the sea is a very long way off.*
Japanese gardener:	*Yes, it is.*
Interviewer:	*Several miles.*
Japanese gardener:	*Yes, over eight kilometres.*
Interviewer:	*That's incredible. Terrible. Are you able to describe to us what happened?*
Japanese gardener:	*We had some warnings, but there wasn't much time. The reports said the tsunami would be a few metres high. When it came, it was a hundred and thirty-seven metres. We were already on a hill, but we climbed up on the roof. At first we felt silly, as if we were overreacting. But even that wasn't high enough. It just kept coming. My friend was as close to me as you are now. I reached out and held his hand. But the water was too strong. He was swept away.*

When Jim woke up, it was as if someone had turned on a light bulb. It wasn't a normal waking up, like a drifting awake where things gradually come into focus.

'Hello there, Mr Barber. How are we feeling now?'

'We? What happened?'

Jim's head was spinning. The man sitting next to him was leaning forward over him. No one had observed him this closely for a very long time.

'We'll get you back to the ward in no time. Just a few checks.'

Jim tried to look around. He could see white walls and he was aware of lights and beeps.

'Your family is all here.'

'All? In that case, I'm definitely dead. You must be the angel Gabriel.'

The man in the green outfit laughed. He told Jim he'd had a bit of a turn. They'd fitted a stent and he'd be on the mend in no time.

But when they wheeled him out through the corridors and into a small room, there they all were: Louise, Sue, even Danny. Louise leapt forward and would have thrown her arms around him but the nurse warned her to mind the tubes.

'Oh, Gramps! What are you doing in *here*!'

Sue came forward, all teary-eyed and cradled his hand.

They all looked in a state of shock.

'Oh, don't look so glum! I'm not dead yet! Danny, you missed your chance, son. I'm sure they could have given me something to finish me off good and proper if you'd slipped them a tenner.'

'Oh, Dad. You daft bugger.'

Sue grabbed Louise's arm and insisted they went to get Jim a cup of tea.

'I don't want any tea!' But they went anyway.

'Wait! What happened to my trees?'

Louise stuck her head back in. 'They're *all* planted!'

'All?'

'All. *And* Dad helped.'

The door slammed and Danny came up to the bed to adjust the pillow behind Jim's back.

'You've changed your tune.'

Danny didn't roll his eyes this time.

'You don't have to be nice to me. They said I'm not dying yet.'

Danny sighed. 'I've only been doing what you taught me to do; bigger yields, more profit, better returns. You wouldn't have planted a field full of cherry trees when you were my age. I just don't understand what you're trying to do.'

'I'm not sure I know either.'

> *Interviewer:*   *So Hanami can be sad?*
>
> *Japanese gardener:*   *There is sadness, of course, but also hope. Only days after the tsunami, when our hearts were broken, the old cherry trees began to flower, even those that had been totally submerged. We couldn't believe it. It was like a miracle. When we saw them we thought, if the trees can go on, so can we; although we refrained from celebrations that year, out of respect.*

It was April. Jim was better. The trees that had been planted the previous autumn appeared to have taken, although they wouldn't be putting on much growth for a while. All of that was happening at root level, out of sight. When Jim first saw them, spaced out in the ground, they had looked worryingly spindly and far less substantial than they had on Louise's computer screen. They'd been planted, according to his plan, in alternate rows of five and seven, 'like a haiku,' said Audrey. Jim didn't know anything about haiku, but Audrey soon explained. That's when she'd visited him in hospital and brought him a copy of a specialist cherry tree catalogue as a get-well present.

It was the same day that Louise had bought him a mobile phone.

'Now you can phone us any time, Gramps. And you can phone your girlfriend.'

Jim was thinking of all these things as he stood at the entrance to the barley field. Not that you could see much of the barley field, or the trees for that matter. It seemed to have been raining for fifteen years. There was a river coming over the opposite hedge where a river wasn't supposed to be. The neighbouring hay field was higher up the hill and the earthen hedge on the boundary was tall, so for a time the water running off the slope had gathered behind it, forming a kind of lake where a lake shouldn't be. This had been a good thing they'd thought, to begin with, to keep the water away from the trees. Until the hedge was breached and the water came over the top in a torrent. In all the years he'd been farming, Jim had never seen anything like it. The forecasters spoke of one broken record after another: the highest rivers, the fastest flows. After a while, the records didn't help.

Jim heard footsteps sloshing towards him. It was Danny.

'Audrey's here.'

'Did she come in a dinghy?'

'She's brought coffee cake.'

'Oh, I like a nice bit of coffee cake.'

'You like Audrey, is what you really mean.'

They stood and stared at the waterlogged field. It was raining so hard that a foot of spray was rising off the ground. The cherry trees seemed to be bowing their heads in shame, as if already defeated. Jim felt sorry for them that they hadn't been planted on a sheltered sunny hill in Japan. Any minute now, he expected to hear the words, 'I told you so'. But instead Danny said, 'It's supposed to be dry tomorrow.'

And, thankfully, Danny was right.

> *Interviewer:* *What comes to mind when you look at the sakura?*
>
> *Japanese gardener:* *Reverence, adoration, appreciation, enjoyment. I also think of awe, fear, and the mysterious and powerful forces of nature. In the West, people think of nature as something that provides them with infinite resources for their well-being. But here, until recent times, there were no separate words for 'nature' and 'mankind'. They were seen as inseparable – parts of the same whole.*
>
> *Interviewer:* *Do you expect to see these trees fully grown?*
>
> *Japanese gardener:* *Ha! I don't think so. The oldest cherry tree is 1800 years old. But it grew at a time when people revered nature. I'm not sure my young trees will be so lucky.*

Jim was sitting in a deckchair underneath the Blushing Bride, which was in full bloom. Eight years on since the planting and for the first time ever, all the perfect conditions required for a spectacular Hanami arrived together. No late frosts, no deluge, no gale-force winds. An area of high pressure and warm wind had eased itself along the Gulf Stream, only to linger over the UK. In a long litany of increasingly erratic extreme weather events, it came as a welcome relief. It probably wouldn't happen again for years, and while it lasted, Jim was going to make the most of it.

The conditions had arrived, and so had the people – hundreds of them, piling out of cars with their picnic baskets and colourful blankets. Louise and Anthony had been promoting the event, building websites and blogs and all manner of things Jim didn't understand.

'They're here, Gramps. Are you sure you're alright to do it?'

'As alright as I'll ever be.' Louise walked back to the yard and soon she returned with the television crew, carrying cameras and sound equipment.

Seeing that his family had gathered to watch, he said,

'You lot can clear off for a start. You're making me nervous. You can watch it on telly like everyone else.'

Jim turned to one of the crew and whispered, 'They will be able to see it, won't they?'

'Of course, on satellite. We'll send you a copy too. It will have subtitles for our audience at home.'

Jim felt more nervous than he cared to admit. His heart was thumping.

They did their sound checks and lighting checks, and then they began.

'Mr Barber, what made you want to plant so many cherry trees, here in the Herefordshire countryside? What was the spark that inspired your journey?'

No one had asked him this question in quite the same way before and it set him thinking, even though he'd prepared his answers.

'Well.'

'Please, take your time. In your own words. We're very relaxed. And very pleased to be here in your beautiful garden.'

Something about her composure made him think of the Japanese gardener. He glanced out over the barley field, which wasn't really a barley field any more.

'Well, you won't laugh, will you?'

'Of course not!'

'It's just that I've never told anyone this story before.'

'An exclusive!' The young woman's eyes glistened and she dipped her head politely as if to urge him on.

Jim told them how he'd gone to pick up rubbish along the road as he often did. It irritated him that the end of their lane seemed to have become a favourite spot for passers-by to chuck any old garbage out of their cars.

That morning, he hadn't gone three yards before he found a crumpled mass of polystyrene packaging strewn along the verge. With his mechanical litter-reacher in one hand and his walking stick and bin bag in the other, he'd picked up the mess and shoved it in the bag. That's when he noticed the half-eaten burger. All this stuff, and they weren't even hungry.

'Perhaps it wasn't very tasty?'

'Perhaps. But a person will eat most of anything when they're really hungry.' Jim thought of his emaciated cousin but this didn't seem like the time to bring it up.

'It preyed on my mind, that rubbish and the half-eaten burger. That was the first spark.'

Then he went on to tell her about the second spark, the programme with the Japanese gardener, that very same evening.

'With Mr Watanabe?'

'Yes. It seemed to me, the longer I listened to him speak, that he and the person who'd thrown the rubbish from their car were totally different creatures. I understood the gardener, even though his language and culture were alien to me, but this other person... well. I know it might seem like a small thing. You could say: how is one piece of rubbish going to destroy the world? But, it's what it stood for.'

'So where do you go from here?'

Jim looked out over the orchard. Although his family had moved off a short distance, they were still lurking. He hadn't noticed it until now, but Danny was holding Louise and Anthony's youngest child, Joshua. They were playing peek-a-boo from behind a rose arch. Baby Joshua giggled every time he caught sight of his great-grandfather. Now you see him, now you don't.

The crew was being very patient. Jim leaned forward and said, more quietly this time, 'You see, when I planted the trees, I had no idea what I was doing. Not really. I just knew that we had to start doing things differently. And I'm not talking about farming here, do you understand? The trees have brought me things I could never have expected, at a time in my life when I thought it was all up.'

'You found your second wind?'

'You could say that.'

'And the future?'

'Carry on breathing. Make people think.'

Interviewer: *And now?*

Japanese gardener: *I will take care of my trees. Keep perfecting the garden.*

Interviewer: *The blossom sustains you?*

Japanese gardener: *Yes. See. Even as it falls, it dances.*

DEAD IN MY TRACKS

On the day of my mother's funeral, an agitated wasp came to harry the bearers. Admittedly, it was an unusually fine day for November, and we were sheltered from the worst of the wind, there on the banks of the river on the outskirts of town. But I'm sure I wasn't the only one thinking, that wasp has no business being out here in the middle of winter. It jabbed at undefended soft parts, mostly the men's ears, one after another, in a methodically vengeful fashion, as if it knew they couldn't retaliate with a well-aimed swipe, given what they were carrying at the time.

Years earlier, a favourite aunt of mine died. She was the gentlest person you could ever imagine. She'd been stamped on by her husband, many times – literally. The day she was buried – in the very same cemetery, as it happened – a spotless white dove came from somewhere and dithered apologetically by the grave. Some of the mourners glanced sideways at each other between hymns and readings. My mother elbowed me sharply, as if to say, 'What do you make of that, then?' When my aunt had told her of the secret stampings, rolling down her support stockings to display the gaudy bruises, my mother had made sympathetic noises, but nothing more. You didn't get involved. Not in those days.

As far as I can remember, nothing remarkable appeared on the day of my father's funeral. However, a few days earlier, before they closed the coffin for good, we paid our last respects at the chapel of rest. Looking at him there, the lines of the last pain still etched on his face, I felt hopeful that Dad was long gone. Only the outer covering was left, dispensed with. By now, he was probably driving his brand new golden tractor in the sky or catching up with old friends in the celestial cattle mart. But just as we were about to leave, a tiny garden spider scurried out from under his neatly buttoned jacket. That suit should have gone to the cleaners, is what I should have been thinking. Instead: spider – of all things! is what I really thought. He'd never been very speedy, my Dad, unless he'd been caught out, exposed mid-field by a sudden clap of thunder, or ducking my Mum's right hook. I raised a hand to coax it away. It retreated double quick, like someone about to be pelted by a hail shower the size of marbles.

Wasp, dove, spider, I'm not passing any judgement here, you understand. All I'm saying is, make of it what you will.

Lately, things have taken a more ominous turn. I was in the kitchen. The patio doors were flung open. A wasp droned in and without thinking, I grabbed a newspaper, rolled it into a lethal baton and despatched the trespassing insect against the double glazing. I scraped up the disarticulated mess, popped it in the bin and returned to whatever job of cleaning I was doing at the time only to be brought to a complete standstill by head-on, overwhelming guilt. Had I just killed my mother? I rushed back to the bin. It was definitely dead. Resuscitation was out of the question. Revisiting the patio doors, I could still see the gruesome smear, the last remaining evidence that it had ever existed. It set me thinking. Since then, several wasps have earned grudging stays of execution, spiders have developed endearing qualities, even the large hairy ones that move disconcertingly quickly when prodded, or threatened with entrapment beneath an upturned glass.

These days are so out of joint. With tiresome regularity, I'm told that things taking place on the other side of the planet are of utmost relevance to me, personally. I am, in some way or other, intimately connected to (and quite likely, unwittingly responsible for) those tragic incidents in Guatemala, Trieste, or Hong Kong. How can I possibly judge myself to be a thinking, empathetic human being without being very, very angry about them. I try my best to be angry, suspecting that the level of observable angriness needs to be perfectly judged.

Exhausted, I've taken to switching off the news, because what really concerns me is the fact that a woodlouse has taken up residence behind the downstairs loo, and the wagtail on the bedroom roof still appears to be without a mate, not for want of trying, and something, unidentified, is living in the gaps between the beams in the spare bedroom, because tiny bits of foam have been chewed and displaced and are now suspended, mid-air on a cobweb ten feet from the ground. It can't be that we were too busy to notice these things before. We were busy it's true; we didn't notice much. But something has changed.

Yesterday, two goldfinches landed on our beech hedge. Only they didn't land in the thicket, the neatly trimmed 'because you know it will only grow nice and dense if you trim it often' part of the hedge, but on the two long wispy extensions, that are supposed, over time, to form an arch, meeting in the middle over a path. The finches faced each other, looking like a prototype design for some heraldic device. Well, how about that, I thought, feeling vaguely honoured that they should have created such a beautiful tableau for my benefit. How lovely. I watched them as they chatted away. They gossiped and turned to glance at me now and then, as if they were passing comment on my outlandish lockdown outfit or unkempt hair. When I made the sound of agreement, they ruffled their wings and shrugged, adjusting their spot as if to say, 'You've had this coming for a long time. What did you expect?'

Sooner or later someone else will die. Where love is unconditional, I'm certain that whatever appears at key moments will make no difference. Flappy ducks? Gregarious geese? Pah! They were kittens with hearts of lions! Neither will we worry about that person who professed profound admiration on all forms of social media whilst busily stabbing us in the back when we were looking the other way. If a snake turns up in the grass while we're reciting the Lord's Prayer at the graveside, so be it. One will accept it with stoicism. Oh, see. There it is. There's that snake in the grass.

But what if the significant event is accompanied by a vision of something that doesn't quite align. What if, at the very moment you hear about the death of a despised old boss on the radio, there appears across your courtyard a cute bunny rabbit? What then? Could one be certain that all that revulsion had been completely justified? Wasn't there just an outside chance that the double-crossing, duplicitous, loathsome schemer had been fluff all along?

There's more. This morning, a high-speed swallow hurtled across the patio and slammed itself into our glass doors. It made an almighty thwack on the window before landing, stunned and twitching on the concrete paving. This is the thing they don't tell you when you're buying floor to ceiling glazing: all forms of bird life will be obliterated by your 'invisible' design statement.

I rushed outside to take a better look. Lying on its side, with only one beady eye visible, it pinned its gaze on me and blinked desperately. I knew what it was thinking. Please, please let the feeling come back to my wings so I can fly away before that massive thing eats me. You don't have to be a bird whisperer to work that one out.

'It's just stunned,' pronounced my husband who'd also heard the thwack. 'It'll be okay.'

I looked down at the quivering creature and wondered how it was possible to distinguish between temporary loss of wing function due to inadvertent collision with immovable object, and actual, final death throes.

'Just leave it be. We'll check on it later.'

It didn't feel right to abandon it there, its little black eye blinking and its wing vibrating with shock, and – most probably – excruciating pain. My husband returned to the house. He seemed hopeful.

'I'll check on you later.' I couldn't leave it without some

kind of rallying remark. At least it was sprawled in a nice patch of sunshine and no rain was forecast.

And then it happened.

I wasn't looking at the swallow, but at myself. I was the stupefied creature who'd knocked itself out, mid-flight, brought up short, just when I thought I was getting the hang of things.

Reluctantly, I went back indoors and we settled down to supper and an evening's viewing of archaeology and ancient history.

Later, on the way upstairs, I remembered the swallow.

'I'm going to check on it. See if it's still alive.' I switched on the patio light and stepped outside. For a moment, I thought I saw it flying off, but it was a skittish bat on its regular evening circuit.

The swallow was gone, and there were no telltale bloodstains or scattered feather-clues as to its fate. The omens were good. I should have been pleased.

'Do you think it flew off?' I asked, climbing in to bed.

I'm not sure why I thought he would know any more than I did.

'Probably.'

'That's good.'

'Either that or it's been eaten by a buzzard.'

My head hit the pillow. I imagined it being gathered up by sharp talons and transported back to a noisy nest where it would be offered up, trembling, to be torn wing from wing by competitive baby raptors.

'We should have looked after it. Made sure it was okay.'

There was a sniff of amusement, and the light on the other side of the bed switched off.

'Mother nature.'

Some mother.

Soon, my husband's breathing became steady and slow.

But I wasn't going to sleep. I was in the buzzard's nest,

high up in the hollow of an ancient oak tree, still aware enough to see four vicious beaks incoming, my one good eye still blinking in disbelief at my inability to fly.

THE LAST FLIGHT OF
LA LIBRAIRIE
D'AFRIQUE DU NORD

Farouk peered out from between the dusty slats. The man was there again, just outside the shop door. It was becoming a regular occurrence. Farouk reached behind the blind, slid back the top bolt, then bent down to do the same with the bolt at floor level, carefully and slowly so as not to aggravate the twinge in his back. Finally, he unlocked the door and opened it as noisily as he could.

A nasty smell filled the doorway.

'You can't stay here. Go somewhere else. There's plenty of other places. Clear off.'

Farouk couldn't see a face. The sleeping bag was like some overgrown caterpillar that was never going to turn into anything nice. The remains of an empty sandwich packet protruded from beneath the grubby navy nylon. He bent down and pulled at a corner of the wrapping with this thumb and forefinger. Something squashed and smelly was left inside it.

'Disgusting,' he muttered, dropping it on the pavement.

He returned to the shop. From a drawer behind the counter, he unwound a black bin liner from a roll.

'You're costing me a fortune. Getting rid of your rubbish every day. Can't you use bins like everyone else? Is that too much for you? You promised me yesterday that you'd find another doorway. You got something wrong with your head? You got Alzheimer's? You're putting my customers off.'

There was a groan, followed by a long sentence filled with swear words. Farouk had never heard a sentence like it. It ended with the words, '. . . you ain't got no fucking customers.'

Farouk picked up the rubbish and put it in the bin bag. He was annoyed. On the way back into the shop, he shoved the door against a bookshelf, completely forgetting that he'd left the metal stepladder there last night. The bottom step jutted out and caught the glass. The doorbell tinkled. A brief wave of intense happiness surged over him, then the entire pane shattered on to the floor. A million tiny pieces spread out in a glorious halo all around his feet.

'What the hell!' Arms emerged from the nylon folds. 'What's going on?'

'Now look what you've done,' said Farouk. It was the first time he'd had a proper look at this slug person who seemed to have adopted his shop doorway as a permanent home. He was young and fair and very skinny.

'You're bang out of order, mate. What about health and safety? Chucking dangerous glass all over my sleeping arrangements. I could have you up in court for assault!'

The young man was on his feet now but the sleeping bag was still caught around his legs as he shuffled around.

'Health and safety? Look at you! You're a disgrace. You've got two arms, two legs, just like everyone else. You're a layabout. Simple as that. You need to pull yourself together. Have a wash. You stink.'

'You got a toilet in there?'

'Course I've got a toilet in there. What do you think I am? Some kind of peasant? And no, you can't use it. Find somewhere else to shit.'

The young man clambered out of the sleeping bag and started walking off.

'What about your mess? You can't leave it here!'

Farouk stared down at the pile of sticky, filthy fabric. What was he supposed to do with it? It was probably the only bedding he had.

'You've got five minutes,' he shouted, 'or it's going in the bin!'

Another string of obscenities came back at him.

He couldn't be wasting his time on vagrants. This was the bookshop's last day and there were things to do. Books to pack. He wished everything could have got off to a more positive start. He'd imagined closing the shop in a blaze of antiquarian glory.

Walking over the threshold, thinking that he wouldn't have to deal with this aggravating person if the electric shutters still worked, the soles of his shoes came to a crunching standstill.

'Oh, the glass.'

'What do you mean, you can't come? I need your help!'

The voice on the other end of the phone was really apologetic. A dance student had been helping him out for the last six months, earning extra cash.

'It's RADA! I can't turn them down. It could be a life-changing audition!'

'And all they give you is an hour's notice?'

'Yes! Well, no. It's a long story.'

'I'm sure it is.'

'Can I come this evening?'

'This evening's no good.'

'You're annoyed.'

'Of course, I'm annoyed!'

'I'm sorry.'

'I'm sorry too!' Farouk pressed the 'end call' button on the handset and threw it across the room. It wasn't his usual way with inanimate objects. He was generally a patient man. Then again, Hannah was usually reliable.

'What's Afrik doo Nord all about then?'

The young man was back, leaning against the doorpost with a can of drink and a fresh pack of sandwiches. He was reading from one of the business cards Farouk had left on the windowsill.

'It's not about anything. It's a place.' Or places, thought Farouk, if he was inclined to be exact about it.

'*Farouk Al...Al...*' He gave up trying to pronounce the surname. 'You wanna sandwich?' It seemed like a genuine offer.

Farouk took in the black fingernails curling around the cellophane. 'No thank you.'

'Good! All the more for me!'

It wasn't said with any obvious malice.

'Once you've eaten your food, you can clear off. I told you, you're putting my customers off.'

The young man bit into a sandwich and made a face.

'And I told you, you ain't got no customers.'

'I have lots of customers, thank you. Online. Anyway, you're in the way.'

'In the way of what?'

'Things. I'll be moving boxes in and out.'

Perhaps the radio would be a deterrent? Which station would be most likely to send the young man packing? Radio 3, he decided. With a bit of luck there would be some Tchaikovsky or some deafening Mahler. He found the radio in the storeroom, under a pile of paperwork. The sleepy-voiced presenter was introducing a recording of a scintillating Proms performance. It just needed to be loud with lots of screeching violins.

He plonked the radio down on a pile of books. As he did so, his shoe caught the corner of a crate. Books went flying.

'You got anger management issues?'

The music started. It was pretty loud. He tried to clear his head and plan what needed to be done next, but over the music he could hear a string of questions.

'Why you selling the shop? You gone bankrupt? How do you make any money out of this stuff? You've definitely got anger issues.'

Farouk grabbed the radio and turned down the volume.

'Hasn't anyone ever told you that it's rude to ask a second question before you've had an answer to the first? You got ADHE?'

'ADHD. Nope.'

All his life Farouk had endured people's assumptions. People were always coming up with lazy ideas about where he was from, what he did, what languages he could or couldn't speak, what strange beliefs he might harbour in his spare time. Why was he always having to explain himself?

'I'll tell you why I'm annoyed. I want to retire. Any objections? This shop has been my life. My parents started it. They came from Marrakesh. They had nothing. Not a stitch. They built it up. They worked hard. They had some books. People passed. They bought and sold. Bought and sold. Sometimes making pennies, sometimes making pounds. They slaved, anyway. Something I don't suppose you'd know anything about. They had pride. They didn't lie about in other people's doorways festering in their own stench. I wanted the last flight of La Librairie d'Afrique du Nord to be dazzling. Now my assistant has rung in to let me down. All this work, and it comes to nothing in the end. Perhaps you're the one who's right in the head. Perhaps I would have been better off lying in a doorway all my life, taking handouts.'

'I've got pride!'

'I'm not talking about you any more. I'm done talking about you! It's not all about you, is it? You want to be a valued part of society, you've got to get up off your arse. You've eaten your breakfast. I've got work to do, and enough problems without being forced to listen to you bleating on and on. Off you go!'

Farouk picked up a stack of crates and dropped them noisily on to another set of crates. Even as he did so, he realised that there was no point to it. He was moving things around just for the sake of it.

'Clear off, I said!'

The young man shuffled off out of sight.

'And take your filthy bedding with you!'

Farouk grabbed a crate, turned it upside down, sat on it and put his head in his hands. He looked at the rows of books on the shelves, all carefully organised. They were like his children. He would keep them all if he could, but the upstairs flat was tiny. That evening, they were all being shipped off to a dealer. He hoped they wouldn't be split into random lots or, even worse, dismembered for their coloured plates.

'I'm sorry I didn't find you all homes.'

As he got to his feet, a glossy turquoise book spine caught his eye. On closer inspection, it said *The Giant Book of Cartoon Fairy Tales*. A troupe of gaudy characters cavorted across the cover.

'How did you get in here?'

He was amazed. He thought he knew every book in the shop. It must be a rogue item in a job lot of antiquarian editions. He examined the garish dust cover. Someone had loved it once because the edges had been carefully sealed with sticky tape to stop them tearing. He looked inside at the publication date. 1971. Magical princes and clever queens danced across its pages in sugar pinks and turquoise blues. In 1971 he had been living with his parents in a temporary house in Casablanca, while they debated whether to make the final momentous move to London. Perhaps his parents had been dreaming of their own fairy godmother at the time?

He placed the book on top of a pile. It was already ten o'clock. He sensed someone at the door and was about to turn around and tell the potential customer that the shop was no longer open when he recognised the footsteps and the shuffle of the sleeping bag.

'Not you, again. What's the matter with you?'

'I was thinking…'

Farouk snorted.

'I was thinking we could help each other out. You need

help to pack and I could do with some cash.'

'Cash for drugs?'

'None of your business.'

'I'm not giving you cash for drugs. Besides, you'd probably steal half a dozen books then disappear. What do you think I am? Stupid?'

'I can pack books.'

'You're filthy.'

'You're only selling them off. Who cares?'

'I care. And that's the point isn't it? That's the difference between us. I don't want your filthy paws on my beautiful books.'

'I can wash. You got a sink?'

'Course I've got a sink.'

'Well. Let me wash, then. I'll help you pack books all day, and you give me fifty quid.'

'Fifty quid! You haven't got a clue! I've worked whole weeks for less profit than that!'

'Thirty, then. I'll help you till it's all done and you give me thirty quid.'

Farouk looked at the shelves. There was no way he was going to get it all done in the time.

'Go on. What have you got to lose?'

Did he have the face of a gullible fool?

'The sink's at the back, by the storeroom. There's a towel.'

Watching him roll up the sleeping bag, something occurred to Farouk.

'Wait a minute. Here's a bin bag. Put your stuff in there. I've got some painting overalls.'

They weren't clean, and they were spattered with dried-on paint, but they were better than what he was wearing. At least they didn't stink.

It seemed to take a long time, whatever was going on at the sink. I must be mad, thought Farouk, and wondered what other disaster would befall him before the day was out.

He could be about to employ a dangerous psychopath for all he knew. Farouk tried to decipher the noises. The taps being turned on and off. The toilet seat being dropped too noisily, the loose toilet roll holder coming off the wall. Something rolling across the floor.

When he reappeared he was dressed in Farouk's overalls.

'Sorry. It fell off the wall,' he said, holding out the toilet roll holder and trailing a black bin bag carrying his clothes and sleeping bag.

'It was loose anyway. That's the least of my worries.'

Farouk noticed that somehow or other, he had managed to wash his hair in the sink. It lay pasted flat on his forehead.

'You should have said, I would have got you some shampoo.'

The lad placed the loo roll holder on a pile of books and picked his way between the crates. He looked much younger with a clean face and Farouk felt a pang of guilt that he might be taking advantage.

'You sure about this? A proper day's work for £30?'

'Yep. You tell me what to do.'

Farouk showed him how to pack the books. He explained about using tissue for the oldest, most valuable ones and how they should be packed spine upwards so that they were easily located, not too many to a crate. He glanced at him often, to make sure he was doing things properly.

'Wait a minute. I don't even know your name.'

'J'

'How do you spell that?'

'J. Like the letter "J".'

'Short for?'

'Short for J. You can't get much shorter than that.'

Farouk was confused. He doubted any parent would call their child by a capital letter.

'Any surname?'

'Not one I'd care to repeat, like.'

He put on some classical music, not too loud this time. They listened to some Bach. Farouk expected J to complain, but he didn't. His incessant questions dried up. Farouk was glad about that.

It got to one o'clock. Every now and again, Farouk would catch a whiff of the stuff in the bin bag. The thought of someone climbing back into them at the end of the day made his stomach heave.

Farouk made his way to the front door, picking up the bin bag as he went.

'I'm leaving you in charge for a minute.'

J hardly replied, just carried on packing.

Farouk hesitated by the door. 'There's no money, or anything here worth taking.' He was banking on the fact that J wouldn't know the value of some of the books.

'I just thought I'd mention it, in case you were wondering.'

J kept on packing. 'A deal's a deal.'

When Farouk returned with sandwiches, but without the bin bag, J was sitting on a crate, engrossed in the pages of a book. I should have guessed he'd be a shirker, Farouk thought, although he was vaguely surprised he was still there at all. He was about to say something along those lines when J said,

'We used to have this book.'

We. It hadn't occurred to Farouk that *he* had ever been part of a *we*. Or that the *we* might have been the kind of people who had books.

'Which book is that?'

J held it up for Farouk to see. It was *The Giant Book of Cartoon Fairy Tales*. He laid the book back down on his lap and carried on turning the pages.

'It was my Dad's.'

All kinds of expressions passed across J's face as he leafed through the stories. Farouk wasn't sure what to do. Was the lad about to have some emotional episode that he, Farouk, would be unable to handle? Would his apparent sadness be followed by anger? Frustration? A violent outburst? J brushed something away from his chin. Was that a tear? Or just dust?

'I bought you some sandwiches.'

J smiled for the first time and put the book to one side.

After lunch, they carried on packing. Farouk checked on J from time to time. He was being surprisingly methodical. Things weren't going too badly, he thought, looking around at the increasingly empty shelves.

The phone rang. Farouk clambered around the books and crates, looking for the missing handset. Why hadn't he put it back in the cradle? The voice at the other end sounded frazzled. Farouk couldn't catch all of it but he did hear the words, 'can't collect' and 'maybe sometime next week'.

'Next week!' he wailed. 'What does that mean? They're virtually all packed.' Then he heard an even more disturbing sentence, which included the words, 'slim margins', 'not enough profit' and 'actually, maybe next month'.

'But we've got an agreement!'

Suddenly Farouk felt the phone being wrenched away from him.

'You're 'aving a laugh, are you? The boss and I've been packing all day 'cos you said you were coming!'

There was a long pause, followed by a lot of random swearing from J, followed by, 'We know where you are. We'll be paying you a visit later. Mr Farouk might look like a nice guy but you won't be messing anyone around once we've finished with you.'

The person on the other end of the phone must have hung up because when J handed it back to Farouk, the line was dead.

Farouk sat down on a box of books and put his head in his hands for the second time that day. Somewhere in the room he could hear a box being pushed along the floor and when he looked up, J was sitting down, also with his head in his hands.

'Have you really got friends who would go round there?'

'Nope. I haven't got any friends. But if I did, they would.'

'I don't think that would solve anything, do you?'

J shrugged and they sighed, in unison.

Just as Farouk was wondering whether anything at all was going to go his way that day, the door flew open. The force behind it, and the loudness of the doorbell, which usually tinkled but always seemed to roar whenever she arrived, could only mean one person.

'See! I made it after all!' There was a crunching noise under Hannah's shoe as she exploded through the door. 'What the fuck? Glass! That's dangerous. Have you had a break-in? Your shutters weren't working, were they? You should clean that up before someone gets hurt.' Before Farouk could respond to any of it, Hannah noticed J.

'Hello! I'm Hannah!' And then, without missing a beat, turned to Farouk. 'You've got a new employee!'

Hannah's smile looked slightly frozen. As well it might, thought Farouk, as he was still quite annoyed with her.

'J's helping me out for the day. Did you get the part?'

Hannah dropped a collection of overflowing bags.

'Nah. They said I was too fat.'

Farouk laughed. He always used to joke that if she turned sideways in the right light, she might actually disappear.

'They wanted someone ethereal and anorexic. I'm not anorexic and I'm definitely not ethereal.' Hannah undid a clip on the top of her head and an avalanche of bright ginger hair tumbled down her back. Then, as if she'd just remembered something, rummaged through the bags and handed one to Farouk.

'The woman at the laundrette told me to give you this.' She turned to J. 'So! What do you do, Jay, when you're not packing books?'

J was still composing his response when Hannah spotted something.

'Oh, my GAWD!'

She leapt across the crates and fell to her knees, gasping dramatically and hiding her face with the palms of her hands.

'My mum had this! Oh, my GAWD, I loved this BOOK!'

She opened the cover of *The Giant Book of Cartoon Fairy Tales* as carefully as if it had been an illuminated medieval manuscript.

'That ballgown! Cinders! Snow White and that gorgeous dark hair. I so wanted her HAIR! Pinocchio and his cute nose... Sleeping Beauty! Her prince was SO handsome. And look – *To dear Iain, with love from Mummy. Christmas 1971.* That's so sad! And now it's here, unloved, in this old place. Can I have it? Buy it, I mean?'

Farouk couldn't help glancing across at J who was sitting very upright but looking distracted and just a little deflated.

'It's sold, I'm afraid.'

Hannah made a face as if to say, I bet it isn't. She was always saying how he loved his books too much to make any real money.

Hannah closed the cover.

'So. What's going on? Why aren't you packing? Has the wine and food arrived?'

Farouk's heart sank. He'd forgotten all about the reception they were supposed to be having that evening for valued customers.

'Well?'

'Mr Farouk's been messed around. The buyer's not coming.'

'Mister Farouk! Ha!' Hannah laughed. Then her mouth dropped open in shock. 'You're kidding?'

'You should keep it open,' said J. He had a mouthful of chicken vol-au-vent so it took Farouk a moment to work out what he'd just said.

'Keep what open?'

'The shop.'

The three of them were perched on crates trying to make inroads into all the food that the catering company had delivered. There were trays and trays, most of them still covered in layers of cling film. Hannah had rung around and cancelled all the guests, on the grounds that there was nowhere for them to stand, now that the buyer hadn't turned up and the shop floor was crammed. Worse still, the heavens had opened outside. Farouk could see water seeping through the layers of cardboard that Hannah had stuck over the broken pane of glass.

'Jay's right. You should keep it open. You'll miss it too much. What else are you going to do with yourself?'

Farouk laughed and rather than answer her question, looked around for his plastic wine glass.

The shelves were empty but he could still see the books: volumes and volumes on peoples, languages, customs, traditions; books on kilims and tapestries, histories of the Berber kings. They were all there, shoulder to shoulder, Syrians, Libyans, Algerians, Moroccans, Muslims next to Christians next to Jews. There were no border checks or midnight raids in his bookshop. Everyone got along in his Maghreb.

'Sod the dealer. Let's give the shelves a proper clean and put the books back,' said Hannah, cutting across his thoughts. 'Listen to that rain! I'm not going home in this. Are you kidding? Anyway, there's loads of food and drink. It'll all go to waste otherwise. And I haven't got class in the morning. We could be here all night. We'll have a ball! Won't we, Jay? And by morning, you'll have a brand new shop. We could even give it a coat of paint while we're at it. Wait! Aren't those your overalls, Farouk?'

'It's a long story,' said J.

'And why is that toilet roll holder on top of an expensive book?'

Farouk poured himself another glass of wine and passed the bottle along.

'Another long story,' said Farouk. His head was starting to swim, and he felt as if he was descending into a fairy tale himself.

'And why did the woman at the laundrette think you were going camping?'

J looked across at Farouk. He had a mouthful of cheese and pineapple by that point so could only make a thumbs up sign once he twigged what had happened to his stuff.

'You guys,' said Hannah, taking the wine bottle and filling her glass. 'What are you like?'

I AM THE MASK MAKER

My name is Francesco da Lucca and I am a maker of masks. This wasn't always the case; not my name, nor my profession.

My father had a modest workshop off Rio dei Santi Apostoli, in Venice. His ambition, beyond creating beautiful cabinetry, was that I should follow in his footsteps, become a master craftsman, like him, and eventually take on his business. At the age of six, just as Palladio was embarking on Palazzo Chiericati, I started at my father's workshop. At that age, I wasn't fit for any real responsibilities. I swept the floors, cleaned the chisels and saws, and was a general dogsbody. I didn't mind it so much. In fact there were times when I almost enjoyed certain aspects. I loved the way the ringlets of wood would emerge from my father's plane, and the fresh woodland scent of the curls would fill the workshop. I loved the way he caressed the sanded joints, and muttered loving words as he ran his calloused hands along a piece of newly polished veneer. Even when the wood had been seasoned for years, it released its secret scent as soon as it was worked: sweet cherry, nutty walnut, warm fireside oak. Sometimes, I wondered if I would ever visit the places where the trees had grown from saplings to ship masts. For the most part, I was content. But it was never going to last. I was always going to be different. A straight road holds no charm for a curious traveller.

At the age of twelve my father asked me to deliver a small chest. Until then, I had never been allowed to go further than our block of streets. He laid fresh woollen padding on the base of the handcart, followed by the chest, wrapped in layers of clean white linen and bound around with plain green cord. Finally, everything was covered with protective leather in case of rain or, God forbid, unfortunate spillages from clumsy, passing pedestrians, or worse still, unspeakable things being poured from upstairs windows.

'Make sure you bow low and respectfully, and wait to see his response,' my father ordered. 'There is more to my business than skill with wood.'

I was too young to understand the meaning of his final comment, and left the shop with the shout to go slowly over the cobbles still ringing in my ears. I made my way through the narrow streets, towards the administrator's house, not far from the Grand Canal.

The door-knocker was shaped like a leaping dolphin. I had to knock several times before someone came to the door, and when she did, the housekeeper looked down at me with matronly disgust.

'I have the chest,' I blurted, completely forgetting the bow, 'from the workshop of Signor Bonario.'

'What on earth are you thinking! Around the back!' and she slammed the door, just as I remembered the bow.

The stone-faced matron was there again as I waited for the master of the house to emerge into the courtyard. I'd taken off the leather coverings to reveal the chest and held them in front of me to hide my quivering knees. I remembered my father's instructions, so when he appeared, I noted his every move. He stopped at the courtyard door. I bowed, wishing I had placed the coverings to one side. I noticed he didn't bow.

He came forward and looked at the chest. Bending down, he ran his hands along the top and sides. He tried to push the lid upwards but it wouldn't budge.

'Key?'

I dropped the coverings.

'A chest is no good without a key.'

I pulled the key from my pocket and nearly fell over him in my haste.

'There are two, sir. One spare.'

'Good.'

I bowed again, just for good measure. The chest opened perfectly, and the rich fragrance of orange wood filled the courtyard. He studied every joint and seam, looking for the smallest defect, while the matron stood nearby, scowling at me as if I'd been a street urchin begging for alms.

He seemed satisfied.

'Tell Alfredo I will send payment tomorrow.'

Not Signor Bonario. Just Alfredo.

I thanked him and left. It was the most momentous thing that had ever happened to me.

The second most momentous thing happened seconds later as I tried to escape the labyrinthine backstreets. I turned a corner, the wrong one as it happened, and caught sight of two people emerging from a tiny doorway. The doorway was inconspicuous, but the two people most certainly weren't: a man and a woman, dressed in the most incredible outfits. The only time I had seen colours like those was at the Basilica dei Santi Giovanni e Paolo one exceptionally beautiful Easter day when the sun streamed in through its magnificent stained glass windows.

I came to a halt because the couple were coming towards me. I wasn't the only one who made way for them. The entire street seemed to pause as they approached like two brilliantly coloured galleons in full sail. Acres of fabric, that would have been considered wholly superfluous to a more utilitarian mind than mine, seemed to billow around them in the shape of sleeves and cloaks and skirts. I gasped, and, in my amazement, failed to notice what they were both carrying. They were only yards away when they brought them up to their faces. This couple, who were already exquisite in my eyes, raised their jewelled masks and were transformed, utterly, from striking humans to earth-bound gods.

Sweeping past, and without a pause in her step, the woman dipped her head towards me, and spoke in the low, musical voice I imagined a goddess would have, and said,

'Amazed, little man?'

Her voice had the hint of a smile in it, so I wasn't offended. But I did close my mouth which, I realised, was wide open. What with the terrifying delivery of the chest and this encounter with visiting deities, my knees struggled to support my body weight out of the shadows of those narrow streets. I pushed my cart past the doorway from where they'd emerged and saw, next to it, a tiny window full of wonders. Just inside the glass, was an ornate mask supported on a stand. I had never seen such a thing. How it was fashioned, I couldn't tell. I doubted it was made of wood. It was inlaid with vibrant turquoise and sparkling stones, edged with the finest fabric and crowned with a plume of white feathers. My mouth dropped open a second time. Why had no one told me these things existed? Why would anyone work in wood when there were materials such as these to be reckoned with? As I stumbled my way home, the cart getting stuck in every rut and gutter, I cursed my lackluster existence.

'The woman's skirt changed colour as she moved,' I told my mother when we sat down for that evening's meal.

She considered my claim, tore a piece of bread in two and dipped it in her thin soup.

'It must have been shot silk: two colours woven together, one in the warp, one in the weft, so that from different directions and in different lights, it looks like two different shades.'

I was amazed that my mother had any practical knowledge of this alchemy.

'Do you have a skirt like that?'

I imagined that perhaps she hid it away and might only wear it on special occasions, of which there were few, I had to admit.

She laughed and turned to my father.

'What use would a woman like me have for a gown of shot silk!' And she laughed again, thoroughly amused at the thought.

I was confused. Why would anyone travel through life, deliberately choosing to turn aside from such delights.

'Besides, it would cost a small fortune.'

She laughed again. Thinking back on it now, it is the most I ever saw my mother laugh at any one time.

The damage was done. It was as if a door had been opened at the end of a dingy corridor, on to a wing of bright rooms I'd never known were there. On my deliveries I would make circuitous detours to the mask maker's workshop. Fridays were exhilarating because the window display would be renewed. One week's mask would have pearls and blue feathers; next week's would have lacquer and multi-coloured beads. I tried to study the techniques, and hazard a guess as to the maker's methods. I was often shooed away.

I struggled on with my apprenticeship, but I had lost all interest. There was a high window next to my workbench and its one peculiarity was the raised level of the street outside. All one could see and hear were passing feet. Those feet came to be a verdict on my unremarkableness; a symbol of how everyone else was exploring the world while I remained imprisoned, as it were, struggling to make headway whilst making dull linen chests for dull city clerks.

In my distraction, one day, I made a particularly poor choice of timber for the base of a drawer; the joints were proving knotty and impossible to work. I hadn't planned to say what I did but the prospect of repeating the work, which was tedious enough the first time around, propelled me into making my declaration. I put down my chisel.

'I can't abide…'

'Abide?' My father raised his head from his latest carving.

'I can't endure…'

'Endure?'

I flinched, and cast around for a more tactful way of expressing my frustration.

'This work is killing me.'

My way with words was no better than my skill with a spokeshave.

Disappointment furrowed my parents' faces.

'What about your father's business?'

We were sitting in the parlour, which was only ever used for visits from wealthier customers. In rejecting the work, it seemed I had already crossed the line from insider to outsider.

My father said, 'Our Lord and Saviour Jesus Christ was a carpenter. If it was good enough for him… '

Ashamed, I studied the surface of the oak table between us and wondered why it was that I should be tormented by this desire to create objects that were of no real use to anyone. Not only was I a disappointment to my parents, but a failure in the eyes of our Redeemer.

Then, my father made an unexpected suggestion.

'I recommend you pay a visit to Our Lady at the church of Madonna dell'Orto and pray for guidance. And when you've done that, come back and tell us what she advises.'

I knelt at the altar. More than anything, I wanted to be a maker of masks. I wanted to be in the world of silks and pearls and gemstones, not in the world of wood. Our Lady gazed down at me with pity, her hand held to her breast as if her heart was already broken by my frivolous fascination.

'Please tell me what I should do?'

I felt that the lack of reply was a reflection on my inability to ask a more specific question, so I tried again,

'I want to make masks but we have no family connections. No one will provide me with an apprenticeship. My father doesn't turn in those circles. He thinks I am wasting my time.'

I persevered.

'I know what I want is impossible, but I will die in that workshop. There must be more for me than this?'

Want, want, want. Our Lady seemed to wince at my self-absorption.

'Please, send me a sign?'

I squeezed my eyes shut, partly to stop the bitter tears and partly to blot out that look of patient anguish. Eventually, I opened my eyes. The blurred scene took several moments to coalesce into focus, but when it did, I found that my gaze had alighted on Our Lady's foot, modestly shod in what looked like a simply painted slipper with no adornment. Of course! My father had a friend who was a shoemaker! He wasn't a mask maker, my profession of choice, but at least he wasn't a dreary cabinetmaker.

I thanked Our Lady for providing the answer and ran all the way home, taking a detour past the mask maker's shop on the way.

I stood in the window and spoke to the latest creation propped up on its gilded stand.

'I promise I will get to you. It's just that I have some things to do first.'

So my route to mask making was becoming circuitous. As I'd hoped, my father persuaded his friend, Bernardo da Lucca, the shoemaker, to take me on as an apprentice. Even though I had to begin again at a lowly level, my enthusiasm for work was renewed; there were many new skills to be acquired, the environment was altogether more inspiring. It's true, we made simple wooden clogs for our poorer customers, (I shuddered at the sight of those chisels and planes) but we also made other footwear: plain leather boots for clerks, velvet slippers for young children, and the occasional pair of brocade dancing shoes with tiny curved heels for the wives of small-time merchants. At last I was learning something about silks and dyes and ornamentation. We worked long hours, carving shoe lasts from beechwood, selecting fabric for the uppers, cutting the designs. I studied the work of my colleagues, no doubt infuriating them with my incessant questions. When something didn't make sense, I would ask why it was done that way.

'That's the way it has always been done,' they would answer. Occasionally, I would make a suggestion, some new technique that might save time or materials, allowing for increased profit. Mostly, they would reject my ideas, but not always. Gradually, they grew more prepared to try things out. They would huddle in a corner discussing the outcome.

'It's not a bad idea. See here, it makes the heel more comfortable.'

What's more, there was a degree of freedom. Merchants' wives didn't want to be seen wandering around the less salubrious parts of town, so we took measurements at customers' houses. By now, I was sixteen and responsible for assisting the master shoemakers on their visits, holding the measuring tape and making a note of requirements in terms of style and colour.

As I arrived one early morning, wondering why on earth I had bothered going home at all as I had only left the workshop a few hours earlier, I stopped to properly examine the contents of our shop window. There sat a pair of workaday clogs, a man's leather riding boots and a sad pair of woman's dancing shoes that were never going to dance a stately pavane, let alone an energetic coranto. There was also a lot of dust. The mask maker's display came back to me and as soon as da Lucca was up and around I approached him with my latest notion, as tactfully as I could.

'Our shop window is dismal.'

'Is it, now?' He sighed. 'What do you propose?'

'I propose we create an exquisite prototype shoe, present it on a bed of velvet and hang a small, lit chandelier above. To attract new passing trade.'

'Anything else, while we're at it?'

'Yes. While we're at it, we may as well paint the window

and give it a good clean. And the door.'

'Who's going to make this delightful knick-knack?' he replied.

'Me,' I said. 'If you will allow me?'

I gave him a list of requirements: stiffened Chinese brocade, gold wire, Flemish lace, white pearls for the centerpiece, the best velvet for the lining, abalone and turquoise for the heel…'

'Stop!' he laughed. 'You're going to ruin me!'

'You won't regret it.'

He knew very well that his account book looked healthier than ever.

'Very well, you can have your materials. But on one condition: there must be *two* shoes, and no fakes; wearable shoes not ornaments. I must be able to sell them, not have them sit in my window collecting dust.'

I agreed to his conditions, but he looked at me much as Our Lady had on that first visit.

'A blessing and a curse,' he muttered, 'the day your father sent you to me.'

That evening I raced to Our Lady to give thanks for her divine inspiration.

News came of a new commission. A merchant and his wife were organising a ball. Da Lucca sent two of us; Grimaldi, the most experienced of all the shoemakers, and myself.

We were shown into an empty drawing room decorated with gilded mirrors and informed that the grandest rooms were on the floors above. Even this first room seemed palatial to us as we waited nervously.

The meeting did not begin well. We bowed low and made our usual deferential noises as the family entered, but nothing could please the lady of the house. She sat sneering as we measured the children's feet. According to her, we were taking too long, not being precise enough, and getting our measurements mixed up.

'Diabolical! What kind of craftsmen do you call yourselves?'

The merchant threw us an apologetic glance.

'Lucilla, please. Let them get on with their work.'

'Oh, yes!' she roared, delighted that his intervention had given her an excuse to vent her annoyance.

'By all means, let them get on with their work! Goodness me, we wouldn't want them to get diverted from that now, would we! After all, no one else around here gets sidetracked from what they should be doing, sneaking off to places they shouldn't be sneaking off to when no one is looking – getting *distracted!*'

She had an impressive pair of lungs and a voice like a fishwife once she got going. I had heard stories of Mount Etna's extravagant eruptions, of the boiling magma and the searing projectiles the size of a house. My colleague and I kept our heads down. Surely, it was only a matter of time before missiles were thrown? The children filed past obediently, proffering their feet and keeping their shoulders hunched in anticipation. The eldest daughter was about fourteen, and gave us a wry smile as she sat to be measured. She presented her foot to my colleague, but pinned her eyes on me. I doubt anyone heard her over the ranting.

'I'm sure your shoes will be handsome enough,' she said. 'But the question is, will they restore my father's reputation, re-instate my mother on to her very high pedestal, and prevent all-round ruination for my family?'

She had no qualms about elaborating while her mother raged on and I scribbled down her measurements.

The wife had been promised a spectacular birthday party, complete with shoes by the best craftsmen in Venice. But the hapless merchant had taken a liking to the shoemaker's wife. The merchant's indiscretion (or more likely, indiscretions) was discovered and the wife's family (who were responsible for funding the merchant's business) duly dismissed the shoemaker amid an avalanche of Flemish lace and a hurricane of freshwater pearls.

Not only was the wife humiliated by her husband's untimely 'distraction', but her long promised outfit (which, incidentally, was more essential than ever, because the shoemaker's wife was younger, thinner, prettier and far less vexatious) was to be utterly ruined for being matched with inferior shoes from an unknown shoemaker who mostly made wooden clogs!

Unless the penitent husband put everything right, with interest, his in-laws would withdraw all financial support. Bankruptcy loomed.

'Will your shoes fix all that?' she teased. Her mother ran out of steam, and my response to the challenge fell on the exhausted ears of a silent room.

'Our shoes will be exquisite.'

'Pah!' screamed the breathless merchant's wife, and the long-anticipated missile, an elegant two-handled vase as it happened, flew over our heads and shattered into a thousand pieces.

Back at the workshop, I addressed the other shoemakers.

'There is more to this business than skill with silk,' I began.

'Oh, here he goes again,' laughed one.

Nevertheless, they laid down their tools and gathered around.

'We must concentrate all our efforts on her shoes.'

'No, no, no!' laughed da Lucca. 'The master pays the bills. His shoes should be the most impressive.'

'Believe me,' I said, 'no one in that ballroom will be more delighted than he when his wife's shoes garner all the attention. And this commission is nothing to what will come later, if we succeed. I guarantee you.'

I repeated what I'd heard at the merchant's house. It all went against the grain, they insisted, but eventually it was agreed, the wife's shoes would take precedence.

While the craftsmen made a start, I visited the windows of other artisans to see about current fashions. They all seemed to follow each other. How were we to make our mark? Whatever they did, I decided, we must do the exact opposite. Everyone should know at a glance that the woman's shoes were from the workshop of da Lucca.

The weeks went by. I had given myself not just one impossible task, but several. I had the usual daytime work to fulfill, the work of an apprentice, made more urgent because of our recent new commission. In addition, I had the challenge of creating shoes for our window display. I stopped going home. Every evening I would sweep the floor and make a bed under my workshop bench.

The day of the ball arrived. We revealed the wife's shoes first. I had made them from the finest Chinese silk and finished them with silver buckles encrusted with tiny beads of glass, each one individually attached with near-invisible wire.

'Green! No one wears *green*!' the woman moaned.

We kept our heads low and didn't rise to the challenge, praying that the shoes would speak for themselves.

One of the little boys gasped. '*And* blue! Look, they change colour!'

'Be quiet,' she hissed. But she hadn't jettisoned them yet, and for as long as she kept looking at them we were still in with a chance.

'Buckles?' she said. 'No one wears *buckles*.'

She turned the shoe under the nearest chandelier and the tiny beads shot beams of light around the dark corners of the room.

There was a small chorus of gasps. 'They make rainbows!' The children danced with delight.

'Do you like them, my darling?' asked the merchant, a little too soon for my liking.

We held our breath.

'The heel is very *low*,' she replied, dubious.

Grimaldi stepped forward and delivered his well-rehearsed speech.

'Everyone knows la Signora is one of the finest dancers in Venice. A high heel would make her unsteady on her feet and prevent her from dazzling the guests with her skill.'

The merchant's 'distraction' had been a poor dancer; this we knew. It was a killer blow. Grimaldi helped her on with the shoes. Once on her feet, she turned a small circle to see how they felt, then doing her best to hide her delight,

'They will do.'

When the payment came, the merchant had added a hefty bonus; such was his gratitude. No one had upstaged the merchant's wife, the dalliance was ended, the shipping loan reinstated, and the merchant's powerful in-laws were happy again.

'You see!' I said. 'There is more to shoemaking than shoes!'

I had also finished the shoes for the window display. Da Lucca turned one of them around in his hands, holding it to the candle and examining it from every angle.

'A blessing and a curse,' he muttered, passing it to the other shoemakers. They said little, but their faces shone with the reflected glow of pearls, and brocade the colour of ripening corn.

'Do they not make you think of the rolling hills of Umbria, on a beautiful late summer's evening, when the earth is warm but the long shadows are elegant and cool?'

I doubt any of the men had ever been to the hills of Umbria. I certainly hadn't. But they smiled graciously and agreed.

'A blessing and a curse.'

A blessing, I hoped. 'But why a curse?'

He laughed, 'I wanted to enjoy the fruits of my modest labour in these final years. But now you bring me this: an unexpectedly dazzling chapter, right at the very end. I believed I was employing a disillusioned carpenter, not some magician!'

We drank a toast to the success of the ball, and to the orders and new commissions that were pouring in. After that, we drank a toast to the shoes that would adorn our new window, the following morning.

For the weeks and months that followed, life seemed perfect. The torments of my past were mostly forgotten. I was content to be a shoemaker and shoemaking seemed content with me. I forgot about masks.

Then, just as the autumn fog descended over Venice, and we looked forward to the new season of events and carnivals, the plague returned. It had called at our doors before, of course, but we Venetians prided ourselves on our ability to stave off its worst effects. In the past, the sick had been routinely removed to the hospital at Lazzaretto Vecchio, where they were cared for without becoming a danger to the rest of the population. When things were particularly bad, ships, cargo and sailors were quarantined in the lagoon for forty days before being allowed to approach the harbour.

These precautions had served us well, and when other cities had been ravaged by disease, Venice had carried on, still trading and making its merchants wealthier by the day. This time, things were different. Perhaps we had been too slow to react? One by one, the churches, the inns, the taverns were closed. Passage over the Rialto Bridge was blocked. People stayed indoors. The city became eerily quiet. My father sent a message to say they had fled to a distant relation in Trieste. Soon there was no one to remove the sick. People died alone in their homes with no one to tend to them.

One morning, as we struggled on with our work, trying not to think about the panic that gripped our beloved city, the notary paid a call. He swept in and out with his scarf wrapped tightly around his mouth and nose, trying not to inhale whatever dangerous vapours might be lingering in our workshop. Within minutes, the owner called me in to his office. Rather than invite me to sit, he kept me standing by the door, which seemed unusually offhand.

'It's been on my mind for a while, although events have rather brought things to a head.'

I had no idea to what he was referring, but I did notice that he seemed uncharacteristically agitated. Tiny beads of perspiration gathered at his hairline.

'You know I have no family to speak of. At least no one who is interested in shoes.' He placed great emphasis on this last word.

'I've left it all to you, Francesco.'

He said many other things after that, but I had difficulty taking them in. He had been like a father to me. I took a step forward, thinking I would at least shake his hand. We had never embraced.

'No!' he said, 'Stand back!' It was clear to me then, that he was already ill. That evening, he took a boat to a nearby island and sent a note. Pray for me, it said, and if you survive, please do me the honour of taking my family name. I ran to the church of Madonna dell'Orto and knelt once more in front of Our Lady remembering how the sight of her neat slipper had put me into da Lucca's path. He had been my blessing, and this curse had taken him away.

I stumbled into the light of the square, desperately sad and hungry. I had plenty of money to pay for food, but there was no food to be had. Many of the bakeries had closed, and even the ones that were open had no bread. Boats were too scared to deliver to Venice and no one could get hold of flour.

Cratefuls of cabbages had arrived at a plaza the previous day and people had descended on them like hungry seagulls. I questioned whether I should have fled with my parents, when there had still been time.

On the way back to the workshop, I saw an appalling scene. A distraught old man on his knees, and a young man, trying to keep his distance.

'Please, Doctor! You must help us!' The old man sobbed.

The young man held a scarf to his mouth and said something about a mask.

'Can't you find a replacement?' cried the old man, falling forward on his elbows.

'The mask maker is dead!' replied the young man. 'Believe me, I want to help you. But I have my own family to think of. I dare not, without a mask. I dare not enter your house!'

The young man stumbled off, leaving the old man weeping and groaning on the ground. I don't know what possessed me to follow the doctor to his house, where, still distressed, he fell against his door.

'Sir?' I called.

'Get away!' he shouted, fumbling with the key. 'I can't help you!'

I didn't need his help, I explained, but I had heard his conversation and wondered whether perhaps he could do with mine?

I didn't go into detail. I described myself as a craftsman, one whose skills could easily be turned to the making of a simple mask.

'But there's nothing simple about it!' he argued, cowering in the doorway. 'It must have a very long beak so that it can be filled with all manner of dried fragrant herbs such as mint, rose petals, juniper berries and camphor. And spices too, to keep out the putrid miasma.'

I had heard of such a mask, but had never seen one. I set

152

to work immediately, following the hurried sketches he had made on a scrap of paper. Even though it was of my own creation, it seemed such a frightful thing, with large haunted openings for the eyes. I could hardly bear to try it on to check the fit. My colleagues shuddered at the sight of me. When I was not in the room, they covered it with a cloth, in case it cursed us all.

When the day came to deliver it, the doctor was so grateful, he offered to pay me double.

'I don't want money', I said. 'All I want to know is where you are able to buy bread and meat and fresh vegetables. We are all starving.'

'In that case,' he replied, 'make me three more for my colleagues, and I will see what I can do.'

Before the end of that week, the shoemakers and their families ate their first proper meal in weeks. The plague had deprived us of da Lucca, but the masks were keeping us alive.

Our workshop was turned over to our new purpose. No one was worried about what they were wearing on their feet any more. Word got around, and soon orders were coming in from other municipalities, as well as our own. Where we could be paid in foodstuffs, so much the better. We made modest profits when other trades were being decimated. Adapting our skills couldn't have been simpler. We had the tools for cutting and stitching leather, and we had plenty of stock in our warehouse for those weeks when the plague-ridden ships arrived late or not at all, because they were detained in some foreign port. The shoemakers' families moved in to the upper floors, believing it to be safer than their own homes. We kept ourselves to ourselves. The streets were unpleasant places to be in any case. People eyed each other with suspicion, looking for telltale signs of fever or nausea or confusion.

The situation went on for months. We began thinking that the world would never be the same. We would never dance a galliard, or meet our friends in Piazza San Marco or see the sun shine through the windows of the Basilica dei Santi Giovanni e Paolo, or see the enigmatic smile of Our Lady at the church of Madonna dell'Orto. We missed making shoes. In the darkest hours before dawn, I even found myself reminiscing about the joys of carpentry.

Then, one day, Grimaldi looked up from our account book and declared with a toothless grin,

'Our orders have dried up!'

We had been so engrossed in our tasks, heads bent low over our benches, devising new ways of making face coverings that were as impermeable as possible, we'd failed to notice that the plague had moved on to torment some other part of the globe. We celebrated for days, and did no work for an entire week.

Life could have returned to normal. Many things did. The families who had lived above the workshop went home. Instead of making my bed on the floor of da Lucca's office I moved upstairs. We returned to being shoemakers and soon the orders came trickling in for wedding slippers and carnival boots.

I should have felt happy, relieved at least. But the plague had planted a new seed of dissatisfaction. I was happy enough overseeing the designs of my colleagues but the work had lost its appeal.

I was packing away the unsold plague masks, and wrapping the last of them in a cotton sheet, when I heard her words, 'Amazed, little man,' as if she had swept past me in the room. Sentimental nonsense, I thought, and went to cover the long leather beak. But as much as I tried not to see its shape, it was still there, under the fabric, bothering me.

I called for one of the men to take the crate away.

'And this one?' he said, picking up the one I'd left on the desk.

'No. I will hang that one on my wall.'

We had a new commission, a recently widowed ship owner's wife, Signora Elvira Solario. I assumed the shoes would be for the funeral, sober and understated. I arrived at her house, tired and bored and wishing I had sent one of my colleagues.

She was diffident and totally uninterested in footwear. She looked away when I measured her feet as if she found the whole encounter distasteful. At my suggestions, she merely repeated, 'That will do.'

I began to pack away my things, when she said, 'Wait. I must also have shoes for a ball.'

'A ball?' I was stunned.

Perhaps she found my reaction impertinent because she felt the need to explain.

'On his deathbed, my husband made me promise to hold a ball.' She searched the floor tiles for some explanation, then added, 'I don't understand. He knew I hated such events.'

The husband had left her in charge of his business: six ships, numerous warehouses and a workforce of cantankerous captains and flighty sailors. They were already proving difficult and demanding.

As I made notes for the evening shoes, I wondered what it was he had detected to place such faith in her.

I packed my things for a second time, and was about to bid goodbye when she picked something up from a table.

'I suppose I must enter into the spirit, as they say, and wear such ridiculous objects.' She brought the mask to her face and my heart sank. It was unquestionably costly and skillfully made, yet clown-like and silly.

'You can't wear that,' I gasped.

She turned to me sharply. 'It was a gift.'

'From whom?' If I was overstepping the mark, I thought I might as well make it worth my while.

She paused, and studied it as if the significance of the answer had only just occurred to her.

'A competitor?' I asked. I could see them, pretending to share her grief when all the while they were waiting for their moment to destroy her husband's achievements. I felt angry on her behalf.

'Yes,' she replied.

From that instant, I knew what had to be done.

I returned to the workshop and gathered my workers around. The mourning shoes and the dancing shoes, I gave others to work on. I told them that no expense should be spared; whatever materials they wanted I would supply. They were to delay everything else and attend only to these.

I removed myself upstairs and began working on the mask. I knew what I wanted. There had to be hidden ribbons and supports so that her hands could be free. I wanted the effect of Japanese lacquer without the long drying processes. It needed to be plain, yet striking, not overworked – the antithesis of what she had shown me. I needed gold.

The days passed, I hardly left the room. The men began to worry. They encouraged me to eat with them. When that didn't work, their wives turned up with pastries and jellies. Some days, they would even bring their children.

'Uncle Francesco!' they would say. 'Why don't you come to the market with us? You need to get away from your bench.'

'The plague has affected him more than we realised,' they would whisper when they thought I couldn't hear. 'How can he tolerate that horrible thing on his wall?'

I didn't have time to explain. All my years of apprenticeship had led me to this one commission. The plague mask was there to remind me that time didn't wait, and chances, when they appeared, had to be taken seriously.

The evening of the ball arrived. Including a humble mask maker on the list of guests would have been considered unthinkable, so I kept on my unexceptional mask and gave a false name at the door. I had never seen so much ostentation.

The light from a thousand candles made everything glow and glisten. The artisans of Venice had been busy for months.

A bell was rung and the guests, who had been mingling, moved into their allotted places. There was a movement at the door to the private apartments, and I saw her rival raising his glass to another merchant. Even though his face was hidden, I could sense his smirk.

The doors opened, Elvira entered and I remembered how we had planned her arrival:

'You must enter in shadow,'

'And I will curtsey here,'

'Just out of the candlelight so that when you rise, and lift your face,'

'I take a step forward, and into,'

'*Light*,'

'And my golden mask,'

'Will make them catch their breath,'

'And I will turn to examine them in a slow sweep, one by one,'

'Considering each one in turn,'

'Whether they have been a hindrance or a help,'

'And when you have registered every last one of them,'

'My eyes will come to rest on him,'

'The *ringleader*,'

'And I will tilt my head, just so.'

'And they will gasp,'

And they did.

Everyone knew the meaning of that look. The sly merchants didn't wait long after that. They made their excuses and left through a side entrance.

The dying ship owner had not underestimated his quiet wife.

At the end of the evening, as I made my way towards the door, Elvira blocked my exit. She curtsied low, extending her silk skirts around her, as if I had been some notable doge.

Then she stood up and, with only a brief moment's hesitation, removed her golden mask. To repay the compliment I bowed and removed my own. The musicians stopped playing.

'Who is he?' they whispered. The guests gathered round.

Elvira smiled. 'Not who, exactly, but what.'

Now the guests were really intrigued. They stood on tiptoes and elbowed each other out of the way for a better view.

Elvira continued, despite my discomfort.

'He is a jeweller, a goldsmith, a carpenter and a master draughtsman. He is also a restorer of reputations, a despatcher of adversaries and an architect of brighter futures.'

These things were not for me to judge. All I knew was that my circuitous path, for all its challenges had led me there, to that time and place, to my name and to my profession; and I was content.

'Who is he?' Someone shouted from the back.

I bowed again, this time to the guests, and replied with the only words I could use,

'I am Francesco da Lucca, and I am the mask maker.'

Background to the cover painting, 'Javi', as described by the artist, David Hopkins

The first thing to say about this painting is that it's enormous, really huge – 2.29 by 1.57 metres (90 by 62 inches). I painted it in 1996. I still think it's a powerful portrait, but it would be a nightmare to accommodate anywhere outside a gallery - it needs a lot of space to be seen! Javi, by the way, is short for Javier.

The painting was conceived as a kind of banner, one of a series (actually the last) of 'heads', like the huge propaganda heads of Saddam Hussein and other dictators that were used in the 1990s, and appeared on billboards and the sides of buildings in Baghdad. My idea was: 'What if we give ordinary people, the individuals important to us, this kind of monumental treatment? They are as important for us, or more so, loom large in our lives. Individuals for us have their own monumentality.' I've since seen other artists do the same in the last 3 decades but not back then when I started doing them.

There were about 10 of these heads, all supersized. And I seem to remember the initial inspiration was from sitting opposite a friend in a downstairs café harshly lit by narrow spotlights from above. For a moment their personality disappeared with the detail of their face, especially the eyes, and I thought 'I have no idea who this person really is, inside.' Disorientating. So that resonated with the 'mask' idea. And then when I worked more on the whole series, I had to think through 'How can I give a chink of insight into who this person is? Or at least presents as being? I think in Shakespeare there's a quote – 'There's no art to find the mind's construction in the face / He was a gentleman on whom I built an absolute trust'. And very influential for me were also the Fayyum funerary portraits from ancient Egypt. They are so powerful. I think you can see ghosts of them in my series of paintings.

It was never originally stretched, nor intended to be, but to be hung from a long batten like a banner. The base layer is the red and yellow vertical stripes of the Catalan flag. Then, on top, the pale turquoise green dazzle of the sea at the beach. Then finally the portrait against the dazzle. Certainly, the idea is there that the person's identity is both there on public display but also hidden, uncertain, ambiguous. So it relates to the ideas of 'masks'. Who knows what other people are really like?

Then in 2017 I found a professional painting conservator and restorer, and paid a lot of money to have it restored. After 25 years rolled up, the paint surface was cracked and flaking - she consolidated it and cleaned it. It had bits of fluff and paint-fragments stuck in the thick oily varnish; she went over it inch by inch with a professional searchlight and removed them! It still had masking tape defining the edges (it was painted on canvas tacked to a huge wall) - I got her to remove some but to keep and glue down the top line of tape. It had to stay because there was one key mark or scribble which careered over the tape and defined the top of his head. Finally, she lined it with another canvas for support, got a custom stretcher made to my exact dimensions, re-stretched and mounted it, leaving the rippled bottom edge free and unattached. The rippled edge still suggests the bottom of a hanging flag or banner. She did a great job. So it was a kind of resurrection.

It was my biggest and maybe most ambitious painting up to that time. Because it's so huge, (it's still just propped against the wall in my sitting room) it's not easy to photograph accurately. The colours are rich though not loud and strong, because the main thing is the contrast of the brilliant light and the face in shadow. It's not anaemic or washed-out in colour. I still have a great attachment to it. It's part of my life history. I said what I wanted to say, in it. And finally, it was actually a good likeness!

I graduated in Fine Art from Central St. Martins in 1996, having also previously studied literature and languages at another university. Basically, I'm a realist figurative painter, and in a way all my paintings are portraits, whether of people, objects or places. Colour and composition are important to me, and my paintings are often slow, needing many layers of checking and refinement.

Though people tend to think I'm typically English, I was actually born in Germany, lived in Gibraltar as a kid, in Italy as an adult and have spent a lot of time in Spain. So maybe my paintings are my space where I can find that something extra to what is: something beyond 'this', 'the everyday'. I guess I'm a shy guy but ambitious for my paintings, and after decades of painting I'm sure of my direction as an artist. I'm making the paintings that I always wanted to.

www.davidhopkinspaintings.co.uk
www.davidhopkinspaintings.com
IG - @davidanthonyhopkins

ACKNOWLEDGEMENTS

I would like to extend a heartfelt thank you to the following: the organisers and judges at Writers' Forum, Frome Festival, the William Faulkner Literary Contest, the Hammond House International Short Story Prize, the Bristol Short Story Prize, the HG Wells Short Story Competition, and in particular Lorraine Mace, Laura Wilkinson, Anita Bryan, Lynn Madden, Ted Stanley, Kate Johnson and Tony Scofield; everyone at Victorina Press, including Pagen Hall, Jorge Vasquez, Amanda Huggins, Sophie Lloyd-Owen and the inspirational Dr Consuelo Rivera-Fuentes; Carl Joice at 4edge Ltd; for the striking cover, Tríona Walsh, Dean Brannagan and, in particular, David Hopkins for allowing me to use his beautiful painting, *Javi*; finally, Liz Evans for proofreading all the stories and for providing so much additional help and support.